INFANDOUS

ELANA K. ARNOLD

INFANDOUS

ELANA K. ARNOLD

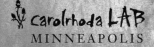
Carolrhoda LAB
MINNEAPOLIS

Carolrhoda Lab™
An imprint of Carolrhoda Books
A division of Lerner Publishing Group, Inc.
241 First Avenue North
Minneapolis, MN 55401 USA

For reading levels and more information, look up this title at
www.lernerbooks.com.

The images in this book are used with the permission of: Emily Harris (wire letters) photograph by © Todd Strand/Independent Picture Service; © Juhku/Shutterstock.com (textured wall); © Odua Images/Shutterstock.com (ripped paper); © A_Lesik/Shutterstock.com (cracks).

Main body text set in Janson Text LT Std 10/14.
Typeface provided by Linotype AG.

Library of Congress Cataloging-in-Publication Data

Arnold, Elana K.
    Infandous / by Elana K. Arnold.
        pages   cm
    Summary: Seventeen-year-old Sephora, a surfer and artist who loves fairy tales and mythology, struggles with a secret so horrible she cannot speak it aloud, especially not to her beautiful, single mother, although they have always been unusually close.
    ISBN 978–1–4677–3849–1 (trade hard cover : alk. paper)
    ISBN 978–1–4677–6180–2 (eBook)
    [1. Mothers and daughters—Fiction. 2. Secrets—Fiction. 3. Single-parent families—Fiction. 4. Sculptors—Fiction. 5. Sex—Fiction. 6. Venice (Los Angeles, Calif.)—Fiction.] I. Title.
PZ7.A73517Inf 2015
[Fic]—dc23   2014008998

Manufactured in the United States of America
1 – SB – 12/31/14

For Rubin Pfeffer,
my agent and my friend

"Everything in the world is about sex,
except sex. Sex is about power."

PART I

Sleeping Beauty

Once upon a time, a great lord was blessed with a baby daughter. He named her Talia, which means "Lamb of God." Desiring to know what her future held, he assembled all the fortune-tellers in his lands. They declared that a splinter of flax would be her downfall. Her father, seeking to outsmart Fate, outlawed the use of flax.

One day, when Talia had nearly blossomed into womanhood, she looked from her window and saw an old crone spinning, spinning. Of course Talia had never before seen such a sight. Her young hand took the spindle from the woman's withered one. At once Talia was pricked by a splinter of flax and fell down dead.

Her poor father, confronted by the inescapability of Fate's hand, could not bear to see his daughter shut into a coffin and lowered into the ground. Indeed, her flesh still bloomed as if with life, though no breath issued from her lips. So he seated Talia on a beautiful throne and left his manor forever.

Time passed, but though the seasons changed, Talia's beauty did not, caught as she was between the flowering of girlhood and the full fruit of womanhood. A trio of fairies visited her often, combing her hair and clearing the sleep dust from her eyes, but otherwise, sleeping Talia was alone. One day, a neighboring king happened by the manor, and as he passed, his falcon came free from his hand and flew up through a window. When it did not return, the king approached the house and knocked on the door. No one answered, so the king followed the bird, scaling the wall of the manor and entering through the window. He trod with reverent caution through the sleeping manor, and he searched each room for his bird until at last he entered Talia's chamber.

Her beauty seemed immortal, but she did not answer when the king spoke to her and did not rouse from her sleep when he ran his finger across her throat. Believing her to be under some sort of enchantment, and beholding her radiance, he felt his ardor stirring. He obeyed its call.

The king gathered her in his arms and carried her from her throne to a bed, where he lost himself in the petals of her flower. When his lust was sated, he returned to his own kingdom.

More time passed—nine months, this time—and, without waking, Talia delivered two babes, one a boy and the other a girl. Had she been awake, Talia would have beamed over their beauty, but as she was not, the children were cared for by the fairies. They bathed and oiled the children and held them to their mother's breasts, where milk flowed even as she slept.

One day the fairies did not come to the manor, and the babes wriggled up like little piglets to the breasts. They searched for her nipples, but one child sucked instead on Talia's finger and drew free the splinter of flax that had pricked her many years before. As if awakening from a restful sleep, Talia stirred and awoke. She saw the two babes and knew them to be her own, though she knew not how they came to be there. She held them to her breasts, and they sucked milk from her and she loved them with her whole heart.

As the harvest moon grew, so did the king's lust for Talia's sweet flesh. Telling his wife he would hunt, he instead returned to the manor. There he found Talia, awake and flanked by the babes. Beaming with pleasure to see the eyes of his beloved, he told Talia who he was and how he had come to find her and how his lust for her flesh had overtaken him when last he had visited. Talia was not displeased by his handsome visage, and this time, when he went to her flower, it opened for him willingly.

When the king returned home, he could not turn his mind from Talia and the babes, and he called out her name in his sleep.

The king's wife, a shrewd and suspicious woman, had felt unsettled since her husband's return from a hunting trip with no game, and she grew doubly so upon hearing the name of another woman upon his sleeping lips. Her jealousy erupted like a pustule, and she sent for the king's manservant and confidant, promising him riches and rewards if he would share the king's secrets and threatening him with death if he would not. Neither brave nor loyal, the manservant told the queen all she wished to know.

The queen, once so informed, sent the manservant to Talia. He told her that the king had sent him to collect the children. When the children were in her clutches, the queen ordered the cook to kill the babes and prepare their flesh in an assortment of delights. The cook could not bear to perform the deed, so he hid the babes and prepared two lambs in a dozen different dishes. The queen herself served them to her husband.

The king ate his fill, tasting each dish and asking for more of everything.

Again and again the queen said, smiling slyly, "Eat, eat, you are eating of your own."

When the king had sated his hunger and had fallen to sleep, the queen sent the manservant to bring Talia next to the palace. He did as she instructed, telling Talia that the king had called for her at last.

But of course it was the queen who awaited Talia, and she unleashed all her fury and jealousy upon her, spitting her accusations—"Whore! Stealer of husbands!"

Talia begged her pardon, claiming her innocence and swearing that the king had entered her when she was not awake, but the queen refused to hear her. She ordered a large fire lit in the courtyard of the palace and ordered Talia to enter the flames.

Talia begged to be allowed to take off the garments she wore, seeking to delay her death at least a moment. The queen, not for pity but rather for greed, gave her permission. Talia stripped herself of her garments as slowly as she could, screaming loudly for help all the while.

At last she dropped her final garment. The queen's servants took hold of Talia's naked arms and began to drag her toward the consuming fire.

But at last the king awoke from his slumber and heard Talia's screams. He ordered his wife's servants to loose Talia and demanded to know where his children were. The queen announced triumphantly that she had had them prepared into dinner and that she herself had served them to the king.

Aghast, the king called out, "Alas! Then I, myself, am the wolf of my own sweet lambs!"

In his fury, he ordered the queen cast onto the flames and listened with grim satisfaction to her screams as her flesh melted from her bones.

The treacherous manservant went next to the fire, and then the king called for the cook. But he appeared with the two babes and so was spared the flames, and the king rewarded him greatly for his cleverness and wept tears of relief to discover that he had not eaten of his own flesh and blood.

And with the queen dead, the king was free to marry Talia, which he did, and they and their children enjoyed long and happy lives, proving true the proverb:

Those whom fortune favors
Find good luck even in their sleep.

One

Things don't really turn out the way they do in fairy tales. I'm telling you that right up front, so you're not disappointed later.

Part of the problem is that we've all been lied to by Disney. You probably know that he whitewashed the shit out of the gory, sexy originals—what, you think a flower's a flower?—that he made them into movies that teach little girls all they need to know to be princesses: be patient, be modest, and above all, be beautiful. If you do these things, Disney promises, then Prince Charming is coming for you and everything is going to work out just fine.

I guess my mom figured things would go down for her like Walt said. She was as beautiful as any princess. The modeling contracts she'd had since she was fifteen attested to that, along with the way the world seemed to rearrange itself to suit her. I've seen the pictures; I would have found it hard to say no too if the teenage version of my mom asked me for something. Hell, I find myself compelled to do the bidding of her thirty-five-year-old incarnation more times than not. But back then—the summer of her absolute apex, the summer when she was seventeen—the world was my mom's bitch.

Her hair, for one thing. I read somewhere that guys notice hair first—before they look at tits or legs or even faces. Hair's the first thing that raises a guy's "ardor." My mom's hair is spun copper. Goldish-reddish, wavy, and gorgeous. That, combined with the fact that her name is Rebecca *Golding*, combined with her modeling and her better-than-average surfing abilities and her willingness to say yes to pretty much any party, at any time, raised her pedestal to break-your-neck-if-you-fall heights.

By the way, who the fuck names her daughter *Sephora*? I'll tell you who. My mother. Golden girl. Fallen angel. Knocked-up model. Unwed mother. She claims she gave me the name because it means "beautiful bird" and "independent," but bullshit. I maintain that she named me after the makeup store. (And another thing . . . about *her* name: Rebecca. I'd bet my ass her parents didn't know its meaning—"beautiful snare"—when they chose it. They probably just thought it was a nice Bible name.)

Anyway, the fairy tale didn't really turn out the way Mom had hoped. The tourist-prince who spread her petals wasn't quite ready for happily ever after, and so he left my mother to bloat and birth all on her own. Her psycho-religious parents disowned her too, kicking her out of the respectable Marina del Rey home where she'd grown up. So she moved down the road to Venice Beach, not far from the break where she'd met my father. When I arrived, it was just the two of us, Rebecca and Sephora, in the first of a string of shitty apartments.

And the rent? (Because shitty apartments aren't free, even for princesses.) No, we're not getting monthly guilt checks from the grandparents. (Though Venice Beach is a convenient place to stash family embarrassments.) Since the last of the bikini modeling jobs ended where the stretch marks began, our life has been decidedly month-to-month. But this is Venice Beach. The math works a little differently here.

**

Right now it's close to midnight on the fifth of June. Yesterday was the last day of school, and that makes me officially a senior now, though the promotion doesn't feel all that thrilling.

But summer is here at least, and I have a week before I have to report to my first day of summer school. Geometry bested me, and now it will return to mock me in the form of six weeks of forced math labor. I decide not to waste another moment of this week thinking about it.

I skate through the mostly sleepy streets of Venice, not the main drag or any of the canal streets, but just through the maze of shitty apartments, a part of town that most of my friends and I call home.

These aren't the streets that Venice is known for. Most people know Venice for its boardwalk, the long stretch of pot pharmacies and pizza joints and tourist traps. They know about the Venice Beach Weight Pen, though most of them call it Muscle Beach, where bizarre, blissed-out steroid junkies pump iron in their tighty-whities, pretending to ignore the steady click of tourists' cameras and cell phones. A few tourists might know a little more—about the three remaining canal streets where the really rich people live. And maybe they know about the web of canals that used to be here, about the ghost pier and torn-down roller coasters and maybe even the camel rides. But our neighborhood—our cheap stucco apartment buildings and dingy drywall caves? Why would anyone want to know about that?

I was planning to sleep over with Marissa, but she got a text from her boyfriend, Sal, that his mom was going to spend the night at her boyfriend's house, so he had the apartment to himself. Marissa and I told her dad that we'd decided to cruise over to my place, and then we parted ways in front of Sal's, her heading inside—petals already spreading, no doubt—and me wheeling solo the rest of the way home.

I have the hood of my sweatshirt pulled up, my ponytail tucked inside. In my loose jeans and black sweatshirt, riding my skateboard, I can pass for a boy. Just in case someone isn't fooled, inside the pocket of my sweatshirt my fingers wind around a can of pepper spray. I flip the safety cap on and off and on again, a habit I've developed.

Lately, I spend as much time as possible away from the apartment, away from its yellowed walls and stained neutral carpet. My mom does her best to make it "homey," as she calls it, but there's only so much you can do with a few well-placed scarves and candles. (Nothing too permanent—like paint or shelves attached to the walls. There's a security deposit to think about, after all.) So my backpack is my home away from home, filled with its usual assortment of supplies: a sketchbook, some charcoals, random food I've scrounged, and, clanking together at the bottom, my water bottle and some things I've collected throughout the day—a few pop-tops, a translucent orange lighter (empty), and a crushed fake-gold earring I found in the gutter outside Sal's house.

It's like this. Sometimes things call to me. Not all things, just some things. And not the things you'd think. Marissa likes to say the things that call to *her* are almost always inside the display cases of overpriced stores, and sometimes she counts on me to distract the salesgirl while she worms her way inside to answer their cries. The things that call to me don't always shine. I do like metal, though, and wood, but I don't consider myself too good for plastic. I've been known to pull things out of trash cans. I've lifted things here and there that had price tags attached to them, but I'm not proud of it the way Marissa is.

Half a moon winks in the sky, providing a little light to skate by but not so much that I feel safe taking my finger off the trigger of the pepper spray. I skate hard in the stretches between streetlamps and cruise in the curved circles of light that they cast. Light to dark to light. And within that rhythm, the regular click of each section of the sidewalk. My mind is everywhere else.

I'm thinking about what I'm going to do with the things I've found. And I'm thinking about Marissa and the way she hooks her index fingers in the front belt loops of Sal's jeans, how he crashes into her when she pulls him by those loops. I'm thinking about something I started that isn't finished yet. All day long I've thought about it—first as I headed to the coffee shop where Carson works (he's always good for a free mocha), and then later as I changed into my bikini to meet Marissa and some other kids for a few hours of R & R. And again as Marissa and I headed back to her place to raid her dad's fridge and sock drawer (beer and pot). I think of the mini blinds on her dad's bedroom window, the way they were angled and the shadow lines they cast. Black bars of shadow slashed across the bed. I think about the shit I had to paw through—some gross porno DVDs, among other things—to find his baggie of pot. Ever since Marissa came across a couple of pretty raunchy girlie magazines one time when she was foraging through his socks and skivvies ("The girls in those pictures don't look any older than us, Seph," she'd said), she's put me in charge of the marijuana-plundering detail. Then we'd headed over to Carson's place with the beer and pot (I owed him after all the early-morning mochas), along with a pizza Darrin gave us out of the back door at the place he works, and the night had ended—I'd thought—back at Marissa's place. Just the two of us again. But stories—and nights—don't always end where they should, so here I am, thinking.

***

Fairy tales are like that. The real ones, the originals, before Disney raped them. The story gets to what you think will be the end—say, Sleeping Beauty wakes up—but that's not the end at all. It's just a reprieve. There's more in store for her, farther to travel, heavier burdens to bear.

But there's my apartment building just up ahead, a dingy, gray-blue rectangular box of stucco and windows and doors and lives all stacked up one atop another. Like it or not, I'm home.

Two

The apartment is dark. I shut the door carefully, not wanting to wake up my mom. The air still holds the scent of the candle she likes to burn. She hasn't been asleep very long.

She has left the door to the bedroom open, of course, though the streetlights outside bathe the room in half-light, even at night. We keep meaning to buy better curtains but haven't yet. When we moved in, there were these mini blinds in the bedroom, but even though they'd blocked out the street-light, Mom had taken them down. Because they were ugly.

That's my mom. Beauty first, then substance.

That sounds really harsh. I don't mean it that way; actually, it's one of the things about my mother that I find endearing, her love of beauty. But it can be annoying when it manifests in Indian scarves repurposed into curtains that don't work for shit to block out the annoying yellow glow of the street outside.

My beat-to-hell laptop is right where I left it, on the far end of our brownish-yellowish Formica kitchen countertop. This guy Tom, who my mom dated briefly last year, gave it to me when he upgraded. It isn't much, but it's mine.

I flip it open and spend a few minutes clicking on random articles that I don't read—I know what I'm doing and that it's a waste of time and that I'm still going to do it—and then a few more minutes scrolling through comments on this art site I like. There's this one duo of artists I think is really amazing. They build these sculptures and then light them so that the sculptures' shadows are thrown on a wall behind them. The sculptures are amazing, but even more incredible is that each shadow is like a whole other piece of art—each shadow image totally different from its sculpture. Like a sculpture of piled-up junk can cast a shadow of a man and a woman embracing. I like what they do, a lot. I've been on this site dozens of times. I'll probably be back tomorrow.

Finally, I go to my art page and scan through some of the images I've uploaded—pictures of my own stuff, a couple things I've built over the last month or so, just the pieces that didn't turn out disappointingly lame. (I hate that artists call their creations *pieces*. It's such a presumptuous word, corny and full of shit. I mean, can't they just call them what they are . . . *products?*)

The worst thing about having a shitty laptop and a crappy connection isn't the laptop or the connection. It's the knowledge that better technology exists. It's the comparison—what I don't have versus what other people *do* have.

I see there's a comment on one of the images I've uploaded, but the photo renders slowly, from the top to the bottom, obscuring the comment itself. I shouldn't care about the comment. Right? I hate that I do, but I force myself to wait while the picture loads, pixel by pixel practically, inch by inch. It's a photo of my latest mermaid sculpture. The core of this mermaid is clay, cheap stuff that self-hardens so I didn't need access to a kiln. She lies on her back, seaweed hair all around her like it's floating. The hair loads first, before her face, before her closed eyes and parted lips. Then comes her neck and then her shoulders and breasts, and I am forced to look at each part separately, my computer stalling out several times. Her arms are spread, palms up. She's a compilation of parts, my mermaid, and as I watch each part appear on the screen, I remember crafting it— the hair, which took three days of gathering, washing, pressing, and arranging, each piece of seaweed spiraled into a separate curl, little pieces of sea glass and shells tucked here and there, like jewels.

The face, which took the longest. Each eyelash is a bristle pulled from a toothbrush I found near the Venice Public Art Walls. I ran the toothbrush through Marissa's dishwasher first, to sanitize it. Then I painted the bristles—one at a time, with the aid of a magnifying glass—all shades of gold. They glisten.

The lips are red wax, molded from an especially lucky find, one of those round wax cheese wrappers. This I plucked from the sand just after Marissa threw it there.

The mermaid's bra is my favorite part, made from over a thousand tiny plastic pellets. They're the number-one source of beach trash, these omnipresent little things, and they're used for manufacturing of all kinds of shit—toys and household stuff and office supplies—and they're terrible, birds mistake them for food and swallow them and then they starve to death. But pressed gently one by one into the receptive breasts of my mermaid, they form an iridescent shimmery bikini.

Everything that adorns this latest mermaid sculpture I collected on the beach. I even incorporated the plastic casing of a hypodermic needle as part of her tail.

At last the bottom edge of her fin loads, the entirety of it uneven bits of sea glass, and with it the new comment.

The comment is just one word—"*Nice*"—and I don't recognize the user name: Joaquin.

Around me, the apartment settles into the next phase of night. I am tired. My eyes burn and my feet ache. Dropping to the couch, I untie the laces of my gray Converse high-tops and kick them off. There is a double bed in the bedroom, but usually either my mom or I crash on the couch. I spread a blanket across it before I head to the bathroom to pee.

I abandon my black jeans on the floor of the bathroom and zip out my hoodie. Dressed just in a tank and my undies, I feel the sharp chill of the beach air through the bathroom's open window, and I hurry to my makeshift bed, pull the quilt up over my shoulder, and press into the back of the couch. That's how I like to sleep—on my side with my back up against something or someone. Until I was twelve or so, I slept with my mom every night, her arms wrapped around me, the perfume of her hair reminding me all night long, even while I slept, that I wasn't alone.

I know most twelve-year-olds don't sleep with their moms. I guess that's why I started sleeping on the couch more often or leaving my mom there if she fell asleep watching TV. But I miss the warmth of her, the way her arm across my body gets heavier when she falls into her deepest sleep.

It's not natural, I think, sleeping alone. I mean, I know most people put their babies in cribs and lots of kids have their own rooms from the time they're born, rooms with doors and locks and skinny single beds. And I'm not saying that I wouldn't like a room of my own—I've actually gone to pretty great lengths to secure a shitty little storage room on the first floor of our apartment building as a place where I can work on my projects—but come on. Do you think cavemen stuck their babies in a separate cave? Of course not. That would practically be *inviting* the wolves—or worse—to come and snack on them.

So even though I mostly sleep alone, when my mom started making noises a year or two ago about getting a set of twin beds, I didn't encourage her. It's nice to know there is still space in her bed for me if I want to climb in.

***

It's weird how sometimes you can't really tell what exactly wakes you up. Is it the smell of the coffee and the sound of it brewing? Or the light slanting though the front window? Or the feeling of my mom's presence, the weight of her taking up some of the space that had been empty while she slept in the next room? Maybe it's all of it, everything together. I open my eyes, just a crack at first and then wider. Mom is sitting at the little round table in the nook off the kitchen, just to the left of the front door. Her coffee steams next to her, and she looks down at the free alt-weekly newspaper she always gets for the sudoku. Her long copper hair is damp from the shower and hangs in a sheet on either side of her face.

She is more beautiful than me. Absolutely, even though I am seventeen and she is twice that plus one more. There is a quality to her beauty, a luminosity, that something special you can't fake. It embarrasses me sometimes, her beauty. Its unnatural immutability. There are other kids with young moms, but no one else with a mom like mine. Really, it's like she is *too* beautiful.

Too beautiful, certainly, to live in this shitty building, too beautiful to have a job as a dental assistant, peering into people's maws, while she works her way, with painful slowness, through nursing school. Too beautiful to wear the awful green scrubs she spends most days in.

I don't mind that she's more beautiful than I am. Because she is beautiful and I am near her, I can look at that beauty all I want. If I were the one who looked like that instead of her, I couldn't enjoy it nearly as much. No one walks around staring into a mirror all day, right? I know her in her entirety. I know where her hair doesn't lay evenly in the back, where a whirl sends one wave in a slightly different direction than the rest. I know where her left eyebrow thins to almost nothing, then picks up again, a tiny fracture caused by a chicken pox scar. I know each fleck in her gray-green eyes. I know her chin, her jaw, her ears, and her mouth.

She must feel me watching her. I blink when she looks up from her puzzle and smiles at me. "Hey, baby," she says. "Sleep well?"

"Mm-hmm." I find that I have sat up without realizing it. Now I stand and stretch. The sky outside the window is heavy with fog, and the light that filters through it is soft like an old photograph.

"Coffee's ready," she says and dips her head back down to the newspaper.

I run my fingers through my hair as I cross the kitchen to the coffeepot. My hair is the same color as my mom's, but the texture is totally different. Where hers is smooth and sleek, mine is a tangle, a mess of waves and curls that doesn't want to fall into a neat style. Where she has one unruly whirl, I have dozens of them.

Three years ago I'd sheared it all off during the first semester of my freshman year. I was in Intro to Spanish with Mr. Gunn, who insisted that everyone call him Señor Pistola. He flirted with all the girls. One day I raised my hand to ask a question during a test—something about subjunctive verbs—and he walked up the aisle, then knelt by my desk. His knee pressed against my foot.

"Señor Pistola?"

"Oh, I'm sorry," he said. His hand snaked out and touched a lock of my hair. "I just can't concentrate when I'm looking at your beautiful curls."

That night I borrowed Marissa's dad's clippers and took it down to the skin, almost. I nicked my head in three places. The long tendrils whispered as they fell to the bathroom floor. My mother cried when she saw what I'd done.

The next semester I switched to French.

My hair had been halfway down my back when I cut it; I'd kept the sides buzzed short but let the middle grow out. Now it reaches my shoulders, but just barely.

Through the kitchen wall I can hear our neighbors' TV. Their kids are watching morning cartoons. As I pour milk into my coffee, I hear a door downstairs slam closed. The clock reads 6:52. Joanne is running late this morning; usually she's on her way to her housekeeping job at the big hotel on the beach by half past. *Housekeeping* is a fancy word for "maid." Once I asked her what the weirdest thing was that she ever found in a room. She said she'd tell me when I'm older.

Mom finishes her coffee and puts the cup in the sink. "I'm going to meet Lucy for dinner after work," she says. "You'll be okay on your own?"

"Uh-huh."

"What are you up to today?"

"Just hanging out with Marissa."

"Going to try to find a job?"

Mom has gotten the idea that I should spend the summer gainfully employed. Things are going to be bad enough with summer school, and since I'm leaving town for a while anyway, visiting my mom's sister and her family in Atlanta, I don't think it makes a lot of sense to fill up the rest of my free time with some lame minimum-wage job.

But we've had this "discussion" before. Mom perceives a lack of work ethic. I explain that I'd rather be broke than yoked. She shakes her head and looks disappointed, and I feel like shit.

Instead of getting sucked into it again, I shrug noncommittally. Mom must not be in the mood for a fight either, because she just sort of shakes her head and drops the subject. She rubs her hand briefly against the side of my head, the part of my hair that is sheared close. She says it reminds her of a kitten. "Okay, baby," she says, kissing my cheek before she reaches for her purse. "Be good."

"You too." I watch her leave through the steam of my coffee; then I slide into the seat she's vacated at the table. It is still warm, the way the bed feels when she's just gotten out, leaving a little pocket of warmth for me to curl into.

The sudoku is complete. My mother's neat numbers—she crosses her sevens—fill each square. Her numbers are like her fingers, her hands, and the rest of her—elegant and ordered, near perfect without effort. I trace her numbers with my fingertip, then flip the paper over to the funnies and run my finger along each comic strip, not really paying attention to the words but instead looking at the color palette each artist has chosen. Some are heavily pastel; others lean toward bright, bold primary colors. A couple of them—those with a darker, more political bent—work in grays and blacks with an occasional fierce pop of red.

My fingers are as colorful as the comics they trace. Layers of paint have totally wrecked my nails, which I wear short like a boy's. Each cuticle is blackened from my charcoals. Red and yellow and green stain my nails and fingers. A thin callus runs down the inside of my index finger, and a matching one mirrors it on my thumb. They are proof of the blade I often hold. Rubbing my finger across them, I can almost hear the sound the blade makes as it pushes through cardboard, through Styrofoam, through whatever I can find, and tears a line. A Band-Aid wraps around the tip of the middle finger of my left hand where I cut myself last week in my studio.

"Studio."

There is nothing neat or clean about my studio, but I can see it all when I close my eyes. A tall table runs along one wall. It is littered with bottles of paint and adhesives; little tins of brushes; stacks of newspapers; markers in all colors, which I've collected since childhood; and coffee cans full of shit I've found, like bottle caps and scratched CDs, little stones and broken cell phone pieces and beach glass. There's a couple of X-Acto knives (the pink one is to blame for my most recent injury), half-empty bottles of glue, spools of tape (thick blue tape, skinnier black electrical tape, and one thinning round circle of shiny gray duct tape), a couple of discarded water bottles, and an old MP3 player (splattered here and there with paint but still functional). There's a stack of whatever paper I can get my hands on for sketching—all the apartment residents hand over their cardboard boxes to me whenever they get a delivery, along with the light brown packing paper that comes inside. A few of the sketchpads I carry with me everywhere (some full, some half full, and one gloriously empty). On the concrete walls are tracings and sketches I've taped up over the last few weeks. They'll stay there for a while, either developing into ideas or eventually disappearing into the bin out back. The biggest pieces of cardboard I've been able to find or forage lean up against the short wall at the back of my little room. Someone two apartment buildings down got a new refrigerator last week, and its box is here now—tall, clean, fresh cardboard, flattened out and waiting for me to cut into it and bend it into something else, something better.

The last of my mother's warmth is gone from her chair, and just thinking about my studio makes me itchy to get down there. I untangle my jeans and shove my legs into them, yank my hair up in a knot, pour myself more coffee with a dollop of milk, and grab a banana before heading out the door, down one flight of stairs, and around a corner.

A humming strip of fluorescence makes it bright enough; still, even with the door open, no real natural light comes in.

But hell, it's mine.

Everything costs something. This small space, one of three

storage rooms off the back alley, cost me weeks of worrying how to approach Johnny, our apartment manager, plus the promise to clean it out—it had been packed to the gills with things former tenants had left behind. Plus, it cost me the two hundred bucks I'd gotten for the one thing in the room that hadn't been a complete piece of shit—a vintage fiberglass Eames chair, sold to the hipster shopkeeper on Electric Avenue. And maybe most of all, it'd cost me pretending not to notice when, as he slipped the storage room key into my palm, Johnny's hand cupped my left breast and squeezed once, hard.

I unlock the door and switch on the light. It stutters into existence in that way fluorescents do, and I step inside. I sip my coffee and look around, then trace my toe along the scratches I've made in the concrete. They form a permanent web, layers and layers of them, sort of beautiful actually, from all the shit I've cut. I set my mug on the table and perch on the room's one chair, a beat-up metal stool. There is no need for a second chair; no one ever comes here.

Then I do that thing I'm pretty good at, from all the practice. I turn my mind away from every distraction—the echo of last winter against my heart; my vague curiosity about how Marissa's night might have gone; my growing irritation over Mom's job nagging, mingled with the impending cloud of doom that hovers just overhead, as summer school ticks closer and closer each second; away from Aunt Naomi's offer, the offer I haven't shared yet with Marissa or my mother. I turn away from all that as I start a playlist and music booms through the small, narrow space. *My* studio. I turn away from all that as I flip through my sketchbook, as I run my finger along a sketch. I've already sculpted this image once; it's displayed in the window of the café where Carson works, though I didn't let them post my name. Now I want to see if I can figure out a way to take this same shape and make it something more, cause it to cast a different shadow.

Three

It's only because this is Venice Beach that Carson's café agreed to put my baby pie in the display case. The sculpture has fluted edges and a latticework crust, just like a real pie, but pierced here and there by the fat arms and legs of well-fed babies, harvested from secondhand baby dolls. People in Venice like the freakish and the odd. They identify with it. A couple of miles up or down the coast, and my pie wouldn't have a place to call home.

The baby pie image has stuck with me. When is a pie not a pie? That's the question I'm playing with, and the answers are pretty funny, right? Like, of course, a flower isn't a flower all the time . . . and then there's pi, the mathematical term, 3.14 . . . et cetera et cetera, and then I'm back to geometry, which, let's face it, isn't all that far away from any sculpture.

I've rotated the table lamp so it throws a shadow on the far wall, and I've been experimenting with different shapes, piling up little empty wooden spools and twisted bits of pipe cleaners stuck together with molding wax. The single bulb pumps out some pretty good heat, and when the morning's fog has burned off, my space grows sweltering. I ignore the first two texts from Marissa, tensing a little each time my phone vibrates, then relaxing again as her name pops up on the screen. But her third text—*Lolly working 2day meet ASAP*—gets my attention.

Our friend Lolly attended Venice High with us until the middle of last year—our junior year—when she decided enough of that shit. Now she works three jobs, all part-time. Marissa and I like it best the days Lolly works at the Smoothie Shack.

Back upstairs I find the green triangle top of my bikini hanging in the shower and a pair of black bottoms in the laundry basket. My gray tee is still clean enough, and I have some cutoff Dickies that aren't too grungy, so I put those on too. Then I slip into my Vans and take my board down to the street.

I pass a few of the local places—there's a secondhand shop that passes itself off as "vintage," a shoe store I can never afford to visit, and a hipster boutique that specializes in ironic eyewear. The shop owners all know me pretty well, and a couple of them let me install some of my art. There's this owl I made from bent spoons hanging in the front window of the hipster place. People can talk all the shit they want about hipsters, but they're pretty cool about making space for local artists.

That owl sculpture—I bought most of the spoons at this one big thrift store where my mom and I sometimes shop. I took the whole stack of them, like twenty-five. And while I was waiting in line, this guy came in. Eighteen or maybe twenty years old. Used up kind of, already. And he tapped me on the shoulder and asked me, "Do you need all of those? Can I buy one?" And I shrugged and said, "Why not?" and gave him one.

Later, when I told Marissa about it, she said he probably needed it to cook his H.

The Shack is on the boardwalk, so I have to maneuver through the tightly packed crowd of tourists. Venice Beach is its own thing. There's nowhere else like it . . . at least, that's what people tell me. I haven't really been many places.

What's funny is that the whole town was built to be like the real Venice, in Italy. It was built by, like, this eccentric millionaire who wanted basically a playground for the rich. It was just a marshland with a pretty three-mile stretch of beach, but enough money can transform anything—at least for a while. The millionaire—his name was Kinney—he had the marshland transformed into a whole network of canals. He brought over actual Italians to give gondola rides. Later, people called Venice Beach the Disneyland of its day. No shit.

But people get tired of everything, and money is fickle and water that doesn't move enough gets fetid and disgusting. Eventually all but three of the canals were filled in, and the whole town turned into a slum.

Marissa is waiting for me in front of the Shack. She has a cigarette tucked between her lips and pulls on it in short, hard bursts, yanking it from her mouth in between each one. Marissa has a love/hate relationship with all her addictions.

"Finally. Fucking around in that storage room again?"

I don't bother answering this. Marissa knows where I've been. "Long night with Sal?"

"Sal can suck it for all I care."

Good to know where they are in their endless breakup-hookup cycle. I don't need any details.

She gives them to me anyway. "I thought it was going to be

just us, you know? Like, for a change? But as soon as we finished fucking"—she emphasizes the word for the benefit of a tourist couple walking by. Melissa takes the obligation to be the local color seriously—"his boy Blake called and cruised over. They spent the rest of the night screwing around on their phones, uploading pictures of each other and calling each other faggot."

"Good times," I say, only half listening. I am hungry. "Is Kayla around?"

Marissa grinds out her cigarette. "Uh-huh. She should be going on break soon."

We wait around for Lolly's boss to exit the building. Marissa keeps herself entertained by rating the guys that cruise by. She has her own rating scale: each guy is assigned a letter of the alphabet. But it isn't *A* to *Z* order—Marissa must have like a touch of autism or something, because she has this theory that some letters are sexier than others. *X*, she says, is the sexiest.

*F*s are pretty hot, and so are *R*s and *J*s and *D*s. If a guy is good looking but clearly not to be trusted, he gets an *S*. Preppy clean-cut types get *A*s and *B*s. Bottom-of-the-barrel types are assigned *P* or *L*, depending on her mood.

"That guy's a full-on *V*," she tells me with a lift of her chin. I follow the trajectory of her gaze and settle on the guy she must mean: he's one of those retro types you see every now and then, with the rolled-up jeans and tucked-in white tees. Pomade in the hair. Tats of brightly colored songbirds.

He must feel our eyes on him because he looks back over his shoulder and smiles. Neither of us smiles back, but Marissa blows a puff of smoke in his direction before grinding out her cigarette. He shrugs, like, *your loss*, and laces his way through a group of the red-eyed stoner kids that cycle through Venice every summer. Last year they had a grungy terrier they took turns pulling around on a rope; this summer the dog is gone.

Finally, Kayla the Bitch pushes through the Smoothie Shack's glass doors, shaking a cigarette from the pack she keeps stashed in her apron pocket. She lights it quickly and slides the lighter back into her pocket, pulling out a phone and narrowing her eyes to its tiny screen as she crosses the boardwalk without looking up once. People shift their trajectories around her. She is like that—not beautiful, but everyone knows to stay the fuck out of her way.

We wait until her head disappears into the crowd on the vast, under-watered lawn just on the other side of the board-walk before we duck into the Smoothie Shack. Lolly is behind the counter, her cute bleached-blonde braids bobbing to the music as she works the cash register and the blenders, dodging back and forth between stations.

"Hey, girls," she calls. "The usual?"

"Thanks," we answer. The people waiting for their smooth-ies look distinctly annoyed that our order has been triaged to the front of the line.

It only takes a minute for Lolly to make Marissa's Passion Fruit and Guava and a minute more for my Berry Blended. She's like a machine behind that counter, reaching for things without even looking first.

It's weird how happy she looks. I mean, it's a shit job—blending up overpriced juice drinks, making in an hour what the total of a single order adds up to. But it doesn't seem to bother her. She likes it—customer service, retail employment. And everyone in there likes her—even as she hands us our drinks before serving the other people who've waited longer, they can't seem to help but smile back at her. A couple even shove dollar tips into the jar on the counter.

"Hey," says Marissa, "text us when you're out of here. We'll meet you."

"Can't," says Lolly. "I'm working the late shift over at Stan's."

Everyone at Stan's Barbecue knows Lolly isn't twenty-one, and technically she's a hostess. But hostesses make shit for tips, so Stan makes an exception for Lolly. She is cute, which never hurts; she's a hard worker, and she never calls in sick. So he just looks the other way when she pops the tops off beers for the patrons and (very occasionally) sneaks a couple of paper-cup margaritas out the back door for me and Marissa.

We wave good-bye to Lolly, elbow-deep in fruit detritus, and swing out of the Smoothie Shack, avoiding eye contact with Kayla the Bitch as she pushes past us, oblivious to anything but her phone's screen.

The day is shaping up to be nice. The June gloom has just about burned off, and it isn't too crowded on the sand. Marissa and I wander over to the playground and sink into a couple of swings, sucking back our smoothies and enjoying the sun on our necks.

"So, you hear from Felix?"

The little hairs on my arms raise up. I am mid-sip and have to fight not to choke on the mouthful of berry slush that suddenly tastes like bile.

"No," I lie. "I doubt he'll call again."

"Huh," says Marissa, watching me out of the corner of her eye as she swings gently back and forth. "Wouldn't have figured that."

I don't particularly want to lie to Marissa. I just don't want to talk about Felix.

"Didja know his name means 'lucky'?" Marissa asks.

"Oh, yeah?"

"Uh-huh. Latin, I think. You know, same root word as *feliz*." She chucks her empty cup in the general direction of a trash can and starts swinging higher.

She is doing it on purpose. Baiting me. Rooting around, seeing if she can get a response. She doesn't know what she's looking for, but she knows me well enough to be pretty damn sure there's something.

"What does *Sal* mean?"

"*Sal* means 'asshole'!" Marissa yells from the very top of her swinging arc. Marissa never misses a beat.

A couple of middle-aged, I've-given-up-on-myself moms start giving us the stink eye, letting us know that the swings are *intended* for their slimy little offspring, not for foul-mouthed teenagers. My god, how they can even stand to live in their skins I will never understand. I mean, I know my mother is the exception, not the rule, but come *on*.

I can tell that Marissa isn't about to give up her swing to the brats, but I stand up. "Come on," I say. "Let's go check out the waves."

***

Not much is happening in the water. The sets are small, one to two feet; every now and then a wave comes in about thigh-high. The lines are mostly walled, nothing to ride.

That's fine with me. I haven't felt much like surfing lately.

I ditch my empty cup in a trash barrel near the biggest art wall. Today is Monday, so no one is painting. I glance over what was painted yesterday—mostly shit, in my opinion. The typical stuff—big letters, heavy shading.

I kind of hate the Venice Art Walls. I shouldn't; I get the point of them—to give people a legal place to make their mark.

But the rules! Ugh.

The short list:

- Painting on the Walls permitted only on the weekend.
- If you're caught painting Monday through Friday, LAPD will slap your ass with a ticket, minimum.
- If you're under eighteen years old, no spray paint. Period. Brushes and rollers only.
- You need a permit to paint.
- You must *wear* said permit at all times while painting.
- You must obtain said permit ahead of time, either in person or online.
- Only three artists at a time can work on the Large Walls.
- Sketches for the Large Walls must be submitted and approved before they can be painted.
- Break any of the rules and LAPD will be waiting.
- All artwork must be completed before sunset. No painting at night. (People only want art made in the bright, healthy California sunshine, I guess.)
- No "Restricted Content" on any of the Walls.

What exactly is "Restricted Content?" Basically anything they want it to be. Profanity, of course, and "gratuitous" violence, anything "too" sexy, anything about drugs or gangs or anything else they decide to deem "graphic" or "obscene." No definitions on the website for the words *graphic* or *obscene*, of course. Nice and vague.

So it's a forum for public art, as long as you play by the rules.

Bullshit.

Marissa knows better than to comment on anything she sees on one of the Venice Art Walls unless she wants to get an earful from me. But today she doesn't seem to feel like yanking my chain; she looks preoccupied.

"Everything okay?" I ask.

"Mm-hmm," she says and smiles at me. Takes my hand.

Her fingers feel warm and strong as they entwine with mine. Her hands aren't stained and cut up; they are clean, her nails even, her skin soft. We walk up the beach a ways like that, swinging our hands comfortably between us.

Sometimes people think that Marissa and I are sisters. We're the same height; facing each other, our foreheads, noses, mouths, and chins match up just so. I know this for a fact.

Her hair is wild like mine, waves and curls and twists, but she's mastered the art of taming it. She's a little more tightly packed than me; her breasts are smaller and tilted upwards; her thighs and butt and back are straight and hard from the years of ballet she did as a kid.

She would probably still be a dancer if it wasn't for tearing her ACL. She's healed from the surgery, and her knee works just fine now and even the scar isn't too huge, but she developed the unfortunate habit of smoking her dad's weed while she was recovering, and she just never got back to those dance classes. She still looks like a dancer, in the same way my mom still looks like a model. There's something about being trained to stand in front of people, the way my mom and Marissa were. It colors everything. Whether they want to be or not, they have been trained to be looked at. They belong front and center.

(You know the term *Achilles' heel*? Like, "He wanted to be a public speaker, but his stammer was his Achilles' heel?" Maybe Marissa's torn ACL is her Achilles' heel. Sometimes I wonder if I'm my mother's.)

I used to hassle Marissa about it, urging her to go back to ballet, but finally she said, "Look, Seph, if it were really important to me, I'd dance. Okay? So shut the fuck up."

So I shut the fuck up. But I notice how she rises up on the balls of her feet while she's peering out at the waves: the triangular line of her calf, her toes turned out, and the straight, smart line of her back.

I ask, "You gonna go back to Sal's later?"

Marissa shrugs.

"I don't know why you spend so much time with him."

Her mouth hardens a little, and she smiles, but not in a nice way. "I guess we don't all have *art*, Seph."

I don't know what to say to this. She seems pissed, but I don't know what about. Her moods sometimes swing too quickly for me to keep up with. Sometimes I want to sculpt her and all her moods—her face, sure, but touched all over with colors, textures. Patterns and shadows and swirls.

It could be whatever went down with Sal or it could be something with her dad or maybe she really is pissed that I've been spending so much time in my studio. I want to ask, but I don't think I'm ready for a big, complicated discussion. The weight of her emotions pulls like an undertow, and honestly, I don't know if I am a strong enough swimmer right now.

Instead of asking, I squeeze her hand. It is code. When one

of us squeezes the other's hand, it means *I love you*. It means *I am here*.

At first her fingers rest just the same against mine. But then she squeezes back.

I let out a breath I didn't mean to hold.

But she isn't going to let me off the hook that easy. "You've been kind of weird, Seph," she says. "For a while now. Is there something you want to tell me? About Felix, maybe?"

There is nothing I wanted to tell Marissa about Felix. I shake my head.

She tries again. "He didn't make you . . . do anything, did he? Anything you didn't want to do?"

I remember everything.

"No," I say. "Nothing. Nothing I didn't want."

Four

At eight o'clock my mother knocks on the door to my studio. I don't hear her at first. My earbuds are in, and I am close to getting something right. I've got a desk lamp set up, and I'm working in front of it with this stuff that's basically Play-Doh, but I made it upstairs in the kitchen, out of flour and cream of tartar and red food coloring. And I'm bending and stretching the lump of it in front of the light, fascinated by the shadow it casts on the concrete wall, its silhouetted fingertips elongated—clutching, spreading, grasping—this hunk of innocuous goo made horrible in the shadow it throws.

My mom pushes open the door, and the warm evening sunlight that spills into my space ruins the effect on the wall. That's how I know she's there. I yank my earbuds out and spin around, my body blocking the lump of dough. "You're home early. I thought you were having dinner."

She hesitates on the threshold, as if she can tell I don't really want her to come in. "Yeah, Lucy got one of her migraines."

"Bummer. Hey, I'll be right up, okay?"

She starts to say something, but then her face softens into a smile. "Okay."

She leaves the door cracked behind her. I close it tight before turning my gaze back to the shadow, back to the form that throws it.

* * *

Mom is in the shower when I go upstairs. She is singing.

When I was a little girl, I used to think that maybe my mother was really a mermaid. I mean, it made sense . . . her voice, her long copper hair. Her beauty, too intense to be mortal, too intense to not be tinged with magic. I did hundreds of sketches of her with a tail.

This was what I imagined:

My mom, Rebecca Golding, was born in the sea. She was the most beautiful of all the mermaids, her hair shinier, her tail shimmerier, her voice more captivating than any other fishgirl's. Her parents were royalty, of course—the king and the queen with all the trappings: a giant gold trident, tall undersea thrones, a beautiful castle made entirely of shells, banners of seaweed waving from every turret.

But she got separated from her family. In my little-girl brain, I watched her chasing a pet sea horse that wouldn't come when she called it, following it farther and farther away until she couldn't find her way home to her shell castle.

The sea grew dark and murky, shafts of light piercing down here and there. She swam and swam, her mermaid tears the same salty water she breathed and cried, breathed and cried.

And then a wave came—boiling, insistent, it bore her to the ocean's surface and threw her far and fast, and she tumbled, head over tail again and again until she landed, coughing and sputtering and drowning in air on the sandy beach. Her body heaved as her tail cleaved into legs, as her lungs drew air.

And that's where they found her—my grandparents, her parents on land. They scooped her up and took her home and never knew her secret mermaid heart.

And she grew up like that, a fish out of water, too beautiful to really pass for one of us. Her hair, even on land, seemed to float as if in water. She moved like liquid gold, crossing her legs, gesturing with long, beautiful fingers, and her mermaid heart beat in her chest all the while.

Maybe that was why they left her, her land parents, my grandparents. Maybe that was why they never wanted to meet me, see me, touch me. Because they had found out her secret— that her tears were ocean water, that she really, truly wasn't of the earth.

And so maybe in a way I wasn't, either. I didn't have her beauty—my hair was frizzy with static, tangled and quarrel-some, not ethereal and floaty like hers. My movements weren't liquid beauty. People didn't turn to follow me with their eyes, not like they did with her.

I drew my mother the way I knew she should look— ephemeral, regal, and free, her skin shimmering into scales at her waist.

What color should her tail be? I tried them all—pinks and purples when I was really young, when those were still my favorite colors. Then greens and blues. Finally, I found the color of her tail when I was twelve years old and made my very first mermaid sculpture, a Mother's Day present that she kept in a place of honor on the fruit-crate bookshelf. The tail was formed of hundreds of newly minted pennies, overlapping like scales. I had taken a five-dollar bill to the bank and exchanged it for five rolls of pennies. I needed clean pennies for my sculpture, fresh ones—before anyone had touched them; darkened them with oily, greedy fingers; spent them; dropped them on the street; stepped on them. Used them up.

Sometimes I still find myself struck by that image of my mother, a mermaid queen, like just now as I walk into our dank little cave of an apartment, as I listen to the rain of the shower and the sound of her voice.

I would do anything to protect my mermaid mother.

Anything.

The place grows quiet suddenly as she cranks off the water. Then I hear someone taking the stairs up to our level two at a time. It's a guy—I can tell by the sound his feet make when they hit the steps.

I am still just inside the door, and it is open behind me. The night is warm, the air wet in that way it often is close to the beach. Outside on the landing the security light glows orange yellow. I can't see who the shape bounding up the stairs will be; in that moment when he is still shadow, still a faceless form, he could become anyone.

Then he reaches the landing, and it's just Jordan.

"Hey, Seph." His hair is wet, like he's been taking a shower too, or maybe he's just gotten in from the surf. The waves were shit today, but that never seems to bother Jordan.

"Hey."

"Your mom home?"

I don't need to answer him because just then the bathroom door opens and out steps my mother, mostly dry, wrapped in a worn gray towel.

Beside me Jordan stiffens. Poor Jordan. He can't help himself. Technically my mom is too old for him, and I know she thinks of him as that kid who lives downstairs, but it is clear as crystal how Jordan feels about her. I can feel it in the air around him, charged.

He's twenty-two or twenty-three, closer to my age than my mom's, but his attention is all in her direction. I can't look away either. Who could?

"Hey, Rebecca," he says. "Sorry to bug you."

"You're not bothering me, Jordan," she says, smiling. As if the sight of her half-naked and wet isn't already enough to ruin him. She has to smile at the poor fucker too. "Give me a minute to get dressed. Okay?"

He and I watch together as she crosses the short distance from the bathroom to the bedroom. Then that door closes and Jordan shakes his head a little, as if breaking from a trance.

"Your mother," he murmurs, but I don't think he really means to say it out loud, so I ignore him.

"Want something to drink?" I go into our little kitchen, more to put some distance between me and Jordan's need for my mother than anything else.

"Um . . . sure," he says. "What have you got?"

Juice, water, some milk. A couple of beers. "I'll take juice," he says. Then, as I twist the cap off the bottle, "No, no, wait—beer."

I don't say anything as I put back the juice, pull out a beer, and knock off its lid.

Jordan takes a gulp of the beer like maybe it'll give him confidence. His eyes keep traveling over to the closed bedroom door.

It's awkward, so I say, "What have you been up to, Jordan?"

It takes a minute for him to register that I've spoken and another for him to form a thought. Finally, he says, "The usual. Work. Surf." Then, to be polite, he says, "How about you? Working on anything new?"

I shrug. "Maybe."

He nods, still distracted, waiting for my mom. But then he says, "Hey. I forgot. My board snapped last week when that big swell came in. Do you want the pieces?"

"Sure. I could at least use the scags."

"I'll put it outside your workshop," he says.

I start to say "Thanks," but then my mom comes out of the bedroom and Jordan's not capable of focusing his attention on me anymore. She's wearing a pair of yoga pants, the plum-colored ones with the fold-over waist that makes like a little skirt, and a black T-shirt.

It is a gray-area outfit. I can't read it, and that frustrates me. If she'd put on a clean pair of scrubs like she sometimes does for nighttime instead of the yoga pants, then I would know that she definitely isn't interested in Jordan. If she'd worn her pink silk wrap skirt, that would have been a signal too. But yoga pants . . . just one step up from sweatpants. A big step, though. Especially with the fold-over skirt thing.

She's left her hair down to dry, and as she walks past me I can smell the jasmine shampoo she uses.

"What's up, Jordan? How are things?" She gets herself a beer from the fridge. I wonder at the possible implications of *her* drink choice.

"Not much. Waves were pretty shitty, but you know what they say."

"What do they say?"

"You know. About a bad day of surfing being better than a good day of work."

Mom smiles. "I don't know about that," she says. "I think work can be pretty rewarding."

I grin on the inside as I watch Jordan backpedal. "Oh, no, yeah, of course, I mean, if you're doing something you love."

"Or even if you're doing something you *don't* love," Mom says, "but you're doing it *for* someone you love."

"Right," Jordan says. He takes a long drink of beer.

I kind of back up quietly, like I'm not there at all, and settle in on the couch. This is promising to be better than TV.

My mom laughs. "I'm just messing with you, Jordan," she says. "I know you love surfing."

He smiles, looking relieved. Until she continues.

"When I was your age, if I hadn't had a kid, I would have spent all my time down at the beach too," she says.

I ignore the twinge this comment elicits in my gut and wait to see how Jordan's going to answer this one. He doesn't, right away. Instead, he leans against the kitchen counter and takes another pull on his beer. I watch my mother watching him, the rise and fall of his Adam's apple, the tanned flesh of his throat. His light brown hair curls against the neckband of his faded-out tee.

"Well, I know all about responsibility," he says, setting his beer on the counter. "I mean, I come from a big family."

A big family. How strange that must be—ours has always

been just the two of us, me and my mom. Once there was a thick letter, addressed to my mom, that I think had been sent by her parents, but she'd scrawled "return to sender" across the envelope and that had been the end of that.

Mom has never offered me information about my father. I have never asked for it. I like the way it is—just us two. I have no desire to share Rebecca Golding with anyone. When I was little and we would sleep together every night, I remember feeling smug. I had friends with two parents, and I knew that their moms didn't hold *them* all night, warm and soft and safe.

Those mothers held the fathers.

Mothers and fathers. I push aside these words, purposefully, and focus on the action in the kitchen.

Jordan is running his fingers through his hair, clearing his throat every thirty seconds or so in between gulps of the beer, which I doubt he is even tasting. I almost feel sorry for him. I mean, you can see that he has it bad—his eyes stay trained on my mother's mouth as she tilts the bottle back, watches as she swallows, as she licks her lips.

I imagine sculpting them—her, a goddess, giant and luminous like the sun, and him, shrunk to the size of a child, gazing up worshipfully.

"So, uh, Rebecca," says Jordan, and I can tell he's winding up for the pitch. "There's this concert next weekend. You know, no big thing, just a local band. I remember you saying how much you like reggae, and I thought maybe you'd want to go." Pause. "With me."

There. I study his face for one moment more—anticipation, eagerness, anxious fear. Then I turn to my mom. *Let him down easy*, I think. After all, he's a nice enough guy and, from an objective perspective, not bad looking, either. Classic California surfer.

But her face is all wrong. She is smiling. And she leans forward in her seat in a way that makes me uncomfortable, in a way that reminds me she has legs where a tail should be.

"Sure," she says. "Sounds fun."

The Rape of Lucretia

The day was filled with bloodshed and cries of rage and pain. With nightfall came respite from battle, and General Lucius Collatinus feasted with his comrades—men with whom he had fought side by side.

They feasted and they drank, and then they rested by the fire. Each man held a goblet of rich, dark wine the color of the blood that had stained the field. They longed for the soft and lovely things of home—their beds and their children and their wives. Far from home, each man aggrandized his wife, remembering her as more beautiful and gentle than she most likely truly was. For women are as men—flawed. No one of them bears a face without a line, a smile without a crooked tooth, a heart without a blemish. Yet, seen from a distance, they can seem as if they do, and that is how it was for Lucius and his wife that evening, the firelight flickering on the bearded faces that surrounded him, causing him to wish more fiercely for the smooth cheek of his wife, his Lucretia.

And with his tongue loosened by the blood his hand had spilled and by the wine in his cup, Lucius spoke of her. He told the men of her beauty, her goodness. Her long, dark hair, which fell in rippling waves to her knees when unpinned. The soft flesh of her thighs, how his fingers sunk into them when he gripped her with passion. Her willing mouth, supple and open to him. And her loyalty—her fierce, unshakable, moral love for him, her husband.

The other men listened. They spoke too of their wives, each in their turn, but none as eloquently as Lucius. Perhaps he had drunk more wine and so spoke more freely than the rest; maybe Death had come closer to kissing him that day than his comrades, and so he waxed more poetically about the stuff of life. Perhaps his Lucretia was a finer specimen of womanhood than the other men's wives. Whatever the reason, Lucius's eloquence captivated one man particularly—Sextus Tarquinius, son of the Roman king. He listened and imagined, seeing in his mind the picture Lucius painted—the flowing hair, the creamy white hip, the willing mouth. Only he imagined himself upon her, not her husband.

No one remembers who suggested it first—that when they returned to Rome, they should travel as a group to surprise each of their wives and see if each was as beautiful and as faithful as her husband extolled her to be.

And when the bloodletting was behind them, Lucius and his soldier friends returned to Rome. One by one they visited the wives of the soldiers, and one by one the soldiers were embarrassed to find their hearths cold and their wives away at play, none of them awaiting her husband's return. Several of the wives were at the homes of their mothers and friends, laughing and drinking in a way that did not befit a wife; others luxuriated at the baths and paid no heed to their mewling children. One was found at home, but tangled in sheets and the arms of her maidservant.

Only Lucretia was where she should be—home, tending the hearth, awaiting the return of her husband. And when he darkened the doorway with his broad frame, she looked up from her needlework with a choked cry of relief, and she stumbled and fell into Lucius's arms, and her hair was dark and soft, and her hips were rounded and supple and begging to be gripped. And her mouth—Sextus Tarquinius lusted for the taste of it.

Sextus Tarquinius left the home of Lucius Collatinus, left the presence of Lucretia, but his thoughts would not follow his form. They lingered, imagining how Lucretia would look as her robe fell away, as her hair came loose and tumbled down, as her mouth opened in a cry of passion.

And though he knew he could not cause her to open to him in passion—for he could see her love for her husband ran deep and strong—he thought it might be enough if she were to open to him in pain.

The next time Sextus Tarquinius knew Lucius Collatinus to be away from home, he visited Lucretia. He went at night and entered her bedchamber while she slept, naked but for the bedclothes. He lowered himself to the edge of her bed and stroked back her hair from her temple, a lover's gentle caress. Slowly, so slowly, he peeled back the linen sheet and feasted on the sight of Lucretia bare to him at last—the slope of her shoulder, the crest of her breasts, and the wine-dark kiss of her nipples. From the bedside table he took a washcloth, dipped it in water, and began to bathe her, trailing the cloth along the curve of her belly.

Lucretia moaned, and her eyes opened, confused at first in the dark, mistaking in the first instant Sextus Tarquinius for her own husband. Who could tell what it was that alerted her to her mistake—to the fact that the man in her bed was a stranger? Was it that his shadow was slightly longer than her husband's? That the fingers pressing into the flesh of her belly were thicker than those she knew so well? Or was it the knife, silently unsheathed, that touched her now between her ribs, its point both cold and sharp?

"Listen now," Sextus Tarquinius whispered between clenched teeth. "I have come to you, and I will have what I want. That is not a question. The question is only if I will have my pleasure with my knife buried in your side or without."

Lucretia made a sound like an animal, trapped and certain of its fate. And then Sextus Tarquinius took what he had come for.

When he left her at last, bereft in her bed, Lucretia despaired that she had allowed him to pierce her with one sword and not the other. Surely the cold steel would have been cleaner, more honorable.

It was a day and another night before Lucius Collatinus returned to his home and his wife. He found her waiting for him, but this time not with open arms and ready lips. Instead, he found her with a knife in her hands. She told him what had been done and who had done it.

And then, with the words, "Avenge me, Lucius," she buried the blade into her chest, aiming the tip just where Sextus Tarquinius had held it not so long before.

Five

Sometimes I can't sleep, but usually I lie there anyway on the couch and stare into the not quite darkness of our living room. Tonight, though, when I find myself awake long after Jordan has gone back downstairs, hours after Mom went to bed, I pull on my pants and walk down to the boardwalk.

It's close to two, the quietest time of the night. The bars are closed, and the drunks have dispersed. The early birds aren't up yet, so I have the streets almost to myself. The homeless, obviously, are out here, but they've curled themselves tight against buildings and park benches, their blankets or jackets thrown over their heads, and they've disappeared inside themselves, become as small as possible to conserve heat, to blend into the night.

I like being alone, and I like being outside in the night air. It's like there is more of it to breathe without everyone pressed around me, competing for it. Venice is a busy city during the day, full of crazies of all shapes and sizes. And the tourists . . .

the never-ending stream of people from all over, coming to Muscle Beach to gawk at the exhibitionists bending and lifting their weights, pressing them up and away with their arms, their thighs, their backs, their muscles straining against over-tanned skin. Exhibitionists, all of them—those lifting the weights and those posing outside the chain-link fence that surrounds the weight-lifting stations. And the girls walking around in their bikini tops and shorts. And the black guys with low-waisted pants and tank tops, headphones slung around their necks, hawking their CDs on the boardwalk. The little families on vacation who come for the day as a break from Disneyland, pushing strollers that are worth more than my mom's car. Rubbing sunscreen on the baby's nose. During shopping hours this place gets packed. Consumers looking to consume, coming to Venice to feast. And us, the locals, the local color, serving ourselves up.

In Venice, money cycles in and out like the tide. People too get caught up in its rhythm, coming back here again and again. My mother says it's all connected—the tide, the cycle of the moon, of a woman.

I think about my mother, the way she smiled at Jordan tonight, and I wonder about men and boys and the gray space in between. It used to be that I enjoyed eyes on me the way Jordan's eyes roamed my mother.

Marissa and I have always made fun of the girls who fuck tourists. It's just too easy to be part of the summer escape, to be the local color that guys go home to tell their friends about—a picture on a cell phone, a text or two, virtual memorabilia that adds up to proof of conquered lands.

No one wants to be the conquered land.

So my first time—not last winter but when I was fourteen—wasn't with a tourist. It was with a boy named Eugene. A terrible name. He wasn't really a local, either. He and his friends used to caravan up to Venice from Orange County every few weekends to skate our park, down near the art walls.

I watched him skate and he watched me watch him skate and Marissa watched us both. "That boy wants you," she whispered into my ear, her breath warm.

Boys want girls. It's just one of those things, not worth questioning. I grew up soaking in it, that desire. Everywhere I'd ever been, men wanted my mother. I knew they wanted what was mine—her touch, her hand, her smile. As I got older, I began to recognize they wanted other things from her, things she didn't even give me, and every now and then, when she gave it to them—never when I was around, but I could always tell from the little scrap of condom wrapper in the bathroom or the salty heavy ocean smell in the bedroom or just the look on her face, later—I hated them. *Hate* is not too strong a word.

That summer, with Eugene, I'd had my period for six months. I knew what it meant—that I could get pregnant. My mother said it meant more than that. She said it meant a fresh start every month, that my blood was a memory of our connection to the ocean, each swell of it moon-born and tidal. I thought it mostly meant a bloody hassle.

Some mothers don't want their daughters to use tampons, afraid that they'll deflower themselves. My mother didn't even keep pads in the house—she had these menstrual sponges, which she rinsed and reused. And she bought me tampons—the smallest size, organic unbleached cotton.

"Your body is yours first," she said. "Don't be afraid to explore it."

Flowers. Deflowering. The tampon box—"Teen" size, it boasted—featured a light pink, open-petaled flower on a baby blue background.

Eugene's penis was way bigger than a teen-sized tampon.

***

I perch on a bench not far from where Marissa and I sat on the swings earlier today. I stare out at the ocean, a booming inky shadow in the night, the crash of the waves louder now than before, now that it's too dark to see them break.

I met Felix out in the water. I was surfing—poorly, since that is the only way I know how. I like it out there, but I'm not a mermaid like my mother. It's just that I like straddling the board; I like sitting under the sun, the rocking ocean beneath me, my legs dangling into the water.

He's the kind of guy who probably doesn't know how to do anything poorly. That was my first impression. I watched him wait his turn in the lineup. I saw how patient he was; even when a kid took off in front of the line, he didn't freak out like some of the other guys did. The kid obviously didn't know the rules; he could barely get up on his board. Probably he was a tourist from somewhere like Tennessee and had no clue there even was such a thing as etiquette. When it *was* Felix's turn, I thought for a minute that he would miss his wave. He seemed to paddle slowly, languidly even, but he must have been really strong, because he caught the wave no problem even though there was none of the frenetic rush that I always felt when I was going for a wave. And he popped right up, clean all the way through, and he handled the wave like *he* was shaping it, anticipating its motion, technical in his ride, carving hard into the surf, his arms almost still at his sides, like he was enjoying himself, sure, but like he was working too, honing a skill rather than screwing around.

I saw him again later as I sat staring out at the sun getting ready to dip into the horizon. He paddled up next to me and straddled his board. We sat there awhile, side by side, not acknowledging each other but just watching the colors from the sunset blend in the water like paint on a palette. It was winter, but it was a really nice day. With the sun going down, though, it would cool fast.

Finally, he spoke. "I didn't see you catch anything today."

"That's because I didn't." I turned to look at him, now that the sun was gone and the sky was that milky-rosy hue. Up close I saw that he was older than I'd figured him to be. Mid-thirties, maybe even older. Brown hair worn short, no gray yet; if he let it grow out, I'd bet it would curl. Hazel eyes, the kind that have lots of colors in them all mixed together, with creases around them when he smiled. Clearly strong but not overbuilt. Not tall, but not short. Too old for me.

But I decided that I wanted him anyway, and so I shifted myself on the board so that the fading light was behind me and I used both hands to wind my hair at the base of my neck, knowing perfectly well that this gesture thrust my breasts out in front of me, pushing them against the sealskin of my black wetsuit, knowing from his gaze that he liked what he saw.

"Sun's down," he said, smiling at me. "Can I buy you dinner?"

We couldn't go anywhere too fancy because all I had besides my bikini and my wetsuit was a pair of jeans, a long-sleeved T-shirt, and two-dollar flip-flops.

He was staying at a hotel not too far away, and we stashed our boards in his room before dinner. He rode an Al Merrick Remix, about six feet long. It was a clean board, pretty new, no dings or repairs. I stood my board next to his in the hotel room, and it looked shameful by comparison: there were about a half dozen yellowed ding repairs and a few more spots that needed attention, and the leash was frayed and tired-looking.

"That board looks too big for you," he said.

"Yeah, thanks, the next time I have a few hundred extra dollars I'll size down an inch or two."

He laughed a little. "Well, considering you spend most of your time out there just floating around, it doesn't matter too much."

His name was Felix. I told him mine was Annie. I told him I was nineteen and finishing up my AA at Santa Monica Junior College. I told him that I lived with three other girls and that was why we couldn't go back to my place. I told him I'd moved to California from Arizona with my friend Marissa who wanted to be an actress and that my job was to keep her from answering any Craigslist postings for "Young Actress Needed/Some Nudity Required" on the days she was feeling desperate.

The only reason I mentioned Marissa at all was because she ran into us as we were heading to dinner. I introduced her as my roommate, and she shook hands solemnly, not giving me away. When we turned to leave, she hissed in my ear, "That guy's an X all the way!"

We had dinner.

He bought a bottle of wine, and even though I might be able to pass for nineteen, I'm pretty sure I don't look twenty-one, but the waitress brought two glasses anyway.

Here's the thing. I have nothing against girls who like to have sex with lots of random guys. That's their prerogative. It's never been my thing, but whatever.

So I don't know what it was that night—the sunset or the wine or Felix himself. But I did go back with him to his hotel, and not just to reclaim my surfboard. I did allow him to kiss me, across my neck and down my shoulder. I did stand still as he slid my jeans down around my feet, as he pulled the strings that held on my bikini.

"I've been wanting to do this all day," he murmured as the bows came undone, first the one across my back and then the other, behind my neck.

No one held a knife to my rib cage. No one made me do anything. I put myself in that room. And when he laid me on the bed, the soft white duvet pluming up around me like a cloud, I wanted to be there.

It was different from how it had been with Eugene, different from how it had been with the other couple of boys I had played around with. With Felix there was this rush of warmth and wetness, this sensation of desire that hit me wavelike and intense.

On that hotel bed, the metaphor felt true, the one promised by fairy tales and tampon boxes. I was a flower and I opened, I softened, and I ripened and warmed. I felt, I thought, like a woman rather than a girl, and as he found his way inside me, I wondered—fleetingly—if this was what sex was like for my mother.

***

And so if I feel like this later, with distance and knowledge I wish I could unlearn, whose fault is it?

There is no one to whom I can appeal, no one to plead for revenge.

I am cold now, dew-damp and tired at last.

Six

It's no big secret that I don't much care for school. My mom knows it; my friends know it; my teachers know it. I do my best to avoid as much of it as possible, and my mom is usually pretty willing to sign whatever sick note I hand her. She hadn't been too head over heels with school herself, she told me, so she totally understands the need to take a day off now and then.

They say junior year is the most important. A formative year, they say. It certainly was for me, but now I'm past it, and I'm not formed into anything I want to be. And now, with summer school, I'm pulled back into the past, repeating something I got wrong the first time.

My desire to *not be here* is so strong it's like a fishing line pulling on my guts.

The only way I can even pretend to stand this is by disappearing.

I flip open my notebook and begin sketching what I see in

front of me—the depressing chalky-green board, Coach Crandall himself in his oversized basketball shorts, his athletic socks and slip-on sandals, his collared Venice High Wrestling shirt, his thick fingers, his bristly cropped hair. I draw it as ugly as it is and disappear.

***

My brain is tired when Crandall finally lets us out, seven minutes after one. It's no oversight, letting us out late. It's his quiet little way of establishing dominance. A few of my fellow losers are going to Taco Bell for lunch. I tag along, more because I don't want to go home yet than because I'm actually hungry.

I order two tacos and water. Then I proceed to transform said water into poor man's lemonade. They have sugar and lemon wedges in the condiments section for the iced tea, next to the sporks and hot sauce. You do the math.

Mackenzie Winters flops into the plastic seat next to me with a sigh. "*Dude*," she says.

I know exactly how she feels.

"How are we going to survive six weeks of that guy?"

I shrug. "The same way we've survived three years of a bunch of guys just like that guy."

She laughs and takes a long drink of her root beer. Mackenzie Winters is a Mormon. She likes to pretend that she is tough, but she won't drink caffeine. And she didn't fail geometry because she skipped class. She failed because she is stupid. Probably she won't fail again because even though she is stupid, she is also rich—at least, rich compared to me—and her dad has hired a student from Santa Monica Junior College to tutor her this time through. He made sure to hire a girl.

Mackenzie sucks at the straw of her actual, bought-and-paid-for fountain soda. I shake the ice cubes in my flimsy plastic water cup and down what's left.

Darrin, the guy with the pizza hookup, is sitting with us too. Pizza delivery boy must not have a GPA prerequisite. He looks downright glum.

"What's up, Darrin?" I ask.

"It's stupid," he says.

I don't ask him to clarify. I get the gist.

After we're done eating, Mackenzie texts her dad to come pick her up. When he gets there, he parks the car, comes inside, and shakes Darrin's hand and mine too.

I can tell he's sizing us up. It's bad enough, probably, that his academically wayward daughter is in summer school; he wants to make sure that she's not hanging out with complete losers. His parental concern is adorable.

Mackenzie and her dad drive off, and Darrin is about to ask if I want to hang out, I can tell.

I ball up the paper wrappers from my tacos and shove them inside the plastic cup. "I'll see you tomorrow," I say.

Darrin gives me a halfhearted wave as I head out the door.

***

The problem is, I don't know where I am going. Not home—our box of an apartment would be frying on a hot day like this. Not my studio—it would be even hotter. I think about dropping by Marissa's place, but she doesn't answer my text, so who knows what's up with her.

Actually, my mom's terrible idea about me getting a summer job is starting to sound slightly less terrible. At least if I find employment somewhere with AC, and if it's a kick-back kind of a job, maybe I can muddle through my mounds of geometry homework in relative peace and quiet. And the idea of getting paid while I'm doing my homework sounds better than *not* getting paid while doing it. If I decide to do it at all.

The flaw in this plan, as I discover over the next few hours, is that not a lot of places want to pay you to sit there. Restaurants I rule out right away—anything in the food service industry is going to mean work and lots of it, the physical kind. Waitress is the kind of job my mom would probably approve of, and it's the kind of job she could walk into any day of the week, if she wanted to. People love to be served by beautiful women—especially here. It makes them feel better. No one wants their burger brought to them by a big fatty or someone with a face full of zits. That's way too real. It makes you think about the burger and where it's going to go after you chew and swallow it, what it's going to do to you next, how your body is going to process it and store some of it and eliminate the rest, through your pores and your asshole. If a beautiful woman hands you your burger, it's like a promise: the burger won't make you fat. How could it, if she's the one to deliver it to your table? It's, like, blessed.

Retail would pretty much suck too. You can't just sit behind the counter and ring up the occasional sale; the owner wants you to wander around the store and offer to help and generally keep an eye on everyone to keep them from pocketing the merchandise. I'd be useless if the store had anything good to sell . . . Marissa would be stopping by in no time, and

I don't think she'd avoid helping herself just because I was on the clock.

And probably I'm unqualified for anything other than retail and food service, which gets me thinking again about what I will do next summer, after high school is over, when a job isn't going to be an *option* anymore.

Even if I did want to go to college, it isn't like my mother has set up a savings account. Either I'd need to take Naomi up on her offer or I'd have to figure out a way to bring in money. Some of the allure of college tempts me, of course—all that potential, balled up into one campus . . . art supplies must be just floating around. But what would be the point? There isn't a career out there that I want, and so far anything I've ever wanted to learn about I've managed fine on my own.

My mother didn't go to college. For the last five years or so she's been working at the dental office, and before that she was a personal assistant for this banker who divided his time between LA and New York. He liked to call her his "West Coast Girl." She organized his dinner parties and picked up his dry cleaning and paid his housekeeper. Before that I'm not real clear on what she did, in the years when I was really little. Service, I imagine.

She would have gone to college, like her sister did, if she hadn't gotten pregnant with me, or maybe she just would have gotten further along with modeling. Hell, we live close to Hollywood; maybe she would have been discovered.

She's taking classes now, of course, working on her nursing career. All of my life, I guess, she's been in the service industry in one way or another—cleaning people's teeth or picking up their dry cleaning.

I wander up and down the boardwalk, asking for applications wherever the uniforms don't look too degrading—a coffee shop, a souvenir store, a couple of pizza places. But I know even as I collect them that I won't be filling them out, and I wonder how my life could be different, what other set of applications I might be able to gather if I had a different life, if I lived somewhere else, if I were someone else's daughter.

Last summer, when my mom first started pressuring me about getting a job, I ran into Eugene at the skate park. I was just getting there, and he was crowding into someone's minivan, heading home.

I don't know why, but my hand shot up in a wave and I called out, "See you next time."

He seemed surprised that I was talking to him. I mean, we'd seen each other a few times after that first time, but I hadn't been very encouraging.

"Probably not," he said. "My dad's making me do this shitty internship for the rest of the summer. Fucking law office bullshit."

He looked genuinely crushed. Me, I couldn't get past the word *internship*.

I'm not far from home, turned away from the beach and the tourists and the crowd, when I slide to sitting. I lean up against a lamppost and try my best to take a few deep breaths. It's close to five o'clock, and the heat is crushing along with everything else. I pull the band from my hair and let my curls flop over into my eyes, offering me some relief from the sun.

I wonder where my mother is.

Have you ever had the feeling that you aren't the main character in the story of your life? That you fill a more minor role—supporting cast, maybe, comic relief, or even antagonist? If that is true—if you aren't the big deal in the story of your life, if your whole purpose is to act as a foil or a catalyst for someone else—then maybe it doesn't matter what you do. Or what you don't do.

Maybe all that matters is what others do to you.

Feet stop in front of me. They are a man's. Worn-out Toms. Tanned, golden-hued calves. Gray board shorts. I look up. "Hey, Jordan."

"Seph, what are you doing?"

"Taking a break."

"From walking?"

"From life."

There's a loose spring on the sidewalk next to my foot. A little one, from a pen. I palm it.

Jordan doesn't know what to say, I guess, because he doesn't say anything, just stretches his hand down to me. I look at it for a minute before taking it. He pulls me to my feet.

"Girl," he says, "you look like fried shit."

He invites me into his apartment to cool down. The shades are drawn, and it's dark. It's kind of loud in there, full of this buzzing humming sound. His place is typical Venice Beach. Shittier than ours, with the window blinds that come standard. Mom is right . . . they are ugly. His place is a studio, and the futon he sleeps on is in the middle of the room, still in full bed mode. I wonder if he ever sits it up. The blanket's wadded down toward the bottom, and there are no sheets. One ugly table lamp and an empty pizza box on the floor. But the air in here is way better than outside, and I sigh with relief.

"Swamp cooler," he says, indicating an ugly metal box

squatting in his window. "My folks picked it up for me at a yard sale. It only works sometimes, though. On dry days. If there's too much moisture in the air, it can't cool things down as well."

His apartment reminds me of a cave—like a rock cave behind a waterfall, with the moisture and the noise.

I flop on one of the two cracked vinyl stools by the kitchen counter. The couch seems too intimate. I shouldn't worry, though. As soon as Jordan tosses me a soda and cracks one for himself, he makes my role clear.

"Did your mom say anything about the concert the other night?"

I shake my head and try not to feel too smug when he looks crestfallen. And I don't tell him what he would like to know—that my mother *always* answers any question I ask about her dates, rare as they are. Most things I don't even have to ask about; she just tells me. Almost always, she is an open book. It's only the big secrets she keeps. So for her to keep quiet about her date with Jordan is unsettling, actually. But I don't give Jordan this information, even though it would cheer him up, make his eyebrows shoot up his forehead in that comical Jordan way. Instead, I crack open my soda and sip it.

The swamp cooler hums. Jordan empties his soda can, smashes it, and tosses it overhand into the recycling bin. Then he says, "I had a really good time."

If I had to guess, I'd say she did too, not only because of her silence on the issue but also because she's been going around humming Rainbow Funkadelic songs for the last forty-eight hours. Another piece of information I won't be sharing with Jordan.

It isn't that I think my mom shouldn't have a sex life. Everyone has one, whether it involves fantasizing to sloppy romantic movies or hooking up with random strangers or dating the same person for years and years. But the thought of my mom with Jordan . . .

Not that minor players have much say in these matters.

But Jordan looks so pitiful sitting there that I can't help but throw him a bone. "Reggae was a good choice. It really is her favorite kind of music."

This cheers him up. "Yeah. She seemed to enjoy it. She danced a lot."

My mother dancing is something to watch. Literally. Everyone stops and watches when she starts to dance. It's that underwater thing again—she moves like a wave, so fluid, her arms and back and hips and legs undulating like she's made not of sinew and bone but of water.

Seemingly satisfied, Jordan changes the subject. "So what are you doing all summer?"

I shrug. "Summer school. Hanging out."

"Doesn't your mom want you to get a job?"

Back to Rebecca Golding. I shrug noncommittally.

"Maybe I can get something for you down at the shop," he suggests. "Like sweeping up and helping with inventory."

Jordan works for Riley Wilson Boards, a local surfboard shaper. A few of the bigger-name surfers ride his boards, including one guy that has a line of board shorts at Target, so the shop is making a name for itself. I've been in there a few times, but really, what's the point? I can't afford one of their boards, and anyway, if I ever have any money, I end up spending it on random stuff for my art.

"What do you do there?" I ask. "Sell boards?"

Jordan kind of laughs. "I'm not much of a salesman," he says. "Naw, I'm a shaper."

"Really? How come I didn't know that?"

He shrugs. "I guess your mom didn't tell you."

Seven

So of course my mom is thrilled that Jordan is going to try to get me a job at the board shop. She comes home looking a little worn out, but as soon as I tell her the news, it's like an extra light gets flipped on. Maybe it's the job prospect that makes her happy. But I don't think it's just that . . . the way she pulls her hair over her shoulder, braiding it loosely and then shaking it out, the way she arches her back to stretch and seems to grow taller, brighter, more alive. . . . No, it's not just the idea of me getting a job. It's that Jordan is getting me one. Because she wants it.

"We should celebrate," she says. When she calls Jordan to invite him along with us, she doesn't have to thumb very far down her recent call list to find his number.

We decide to go out for Chinese, and my mom disappears into the bedroom to get ready. She skips a shower to give me time to take one, and feeling sullied by the hot day, my job hunt, and summer school, I do the whole thing—shampoo, conditioner, body wash, and shaving—all of it.

I'm not the kind of girl who gets lost in the shower, the way my mother does. She practically moves into the bathroom sometimes, lighting candles and oiling her bathwater, putting on just the right music. It's like she's romancing herself, the way she tends to her body.

My mother helped me shave my legs for the first time at thirteen. All my life, I had watched her shave hers—unbroken strokes from ankle to hip, sliding the razor across the bend of her knee, up her thigh, unflinching. The oil she used, the razor—an old-fashioned man's razor, heavy and silver, with replaceable blades—not a pink plastic "women's" safety razor. The way she sat in the bathtub and balanced her toes on the edge of the sink, pearlescent toenails like seashells all in a row.

She bought me a pack of three safety razors. "There is nothing wrong with the hair on your legs," she told me one last time, almost like she hoped I'd change my mind, but when I rolled my eyes and said nothing she sighed and broke open the package.

"Always soak first," she said. "Use warm water, and don't press too hard. Okay?"

I sat in the bathtub, the water made murky by the oil she'd dripped in. I was naked. I remember the razor in her right hand. She kneeled by the tub and held my foot in her left hand. She pressed the blade just above my ankle. She paused, waiting for me.

"Okay," I said, and I watched her hand guide the razor up my leg, scraping away the cream she'd rubbed on, leaving behind a shiny trail of hairless skin. It was beautiful.

"Now you try," she said and handed me the razor. "Be gentle with yourself."

As I shaved, one row and then another and then another, she sat on the floor of our tiny, steamed bathroom and gazed up at the ceiling. She was wearing this long silk patchwork skirt, and she ran her fingers along its hem as if looking for some answer in the stitches. She was in a nostalgic mood, I could tell. Then she said, "My mother didn't let me shave my legs until I was sixteen. And she told me never to shave above my knees. Of course I didn't listen to her."

I traced the razor along my knee and then above, shaving all the way to the top of my thigh.

"I got pregnant with you thirteen months after I started shaving my legs," she said with a smile. "That's what I get for shaving above my knees, I guess."

The razor slipped a little on my next pass across my anklebone, and I felt the sharp sting of cutting myself. A thin red line appeared where the razor had cut me, just a tiny thing. I splashed water over it and the blood went way, but it came back.

My mother didn't notice. She stood and kissed my hair. "Best decision I ever made," she said before she left the bathroom, leaving me to finish my legs. She didn't say which decision.

Now, I am efficient. I shave in the shower, standing up, my leg against the wall. Short strokes. Like sketching. Sometimes I spread some shampoo across my skin before I shave, but that's about as fancy as I get.

I don't know why I'm in such a good mood when I emerge from the bathroom. Maybe it's the prospect of the spending money a job would generate. Whatever it is, I'm actually not too annoyed when I emerge from the bathroom to find my mother wearing her red silk dress.

Now, normally it would be pretty stale to wear a Chinese dress to a Chinese restaurant, especially if you're not actually Chinese. But my mom can pull it off. She's had the dress for years. She picked it up at a thrift shop, and it's one of those long, straight column dresses that doesn't fit anybody right because it's got these darts on the chest, and on lots of women those either hang like limp pockets or cut across the boobs all funny. But my mom isn't anybody.

The dress is also sleeveless with a deep slit up the right side.

I mean, come on. Right?

But the thing is, my mother looks . . . charming in it. And with her long copper hair in loose waves down her back and her amazing lips darkened to red, she is so beautiful. Not ironic or anything.

My first thought isn't that she is dressing up for Jordan. Because my mom and I, whenever we go out to celebrate anything, she's always dressed up. Always. And I used to as well. I'm not really sure when I stopped or why. It has something to do with how uncomfortable I began to feel about people looking at me. It used to be that I was like an extension of my mother. I mean, she was the showstopper. I was just this goofy kid hanging on her arm, wearing a dress in a color that matched hers, but not the main point, you know.

Then I got older. And still, my mother was the star of every outing, but rather than an accessory, I became more of a sidekick, and people started saying things like, "Watch out! This one's going to be trouble!" and "She's going to grow up to be a heartbreaker, same as her mama!"

And like I said before, I don't particularly like attention. Not that kind of attention. Plus, all these strangers who seemed to feel that they had the right to comment on us, they had it all wrong. I'd never seen my mother break anyone's heart. I certainly had no intention of ever doing so. We had between us two whole hearts, and back then, as far as I knew, that was plenty for both of us.

***

Jordan is predictably impressed by my mother's red dress. He says, "You look nice, Seph," but without really looking at me. The way he looks at *her*—the intensity of his desire—almost makes me lose my appetite.

Almost. The promise of kung pao chicken has a way of rectifying most things.

***

The restaurant is packed, but that doesn't matter. We're with Rebecca Golding, and even waiting for a table is good times. The whole place comes alive when we walk in, and it goes from being this disparate collection of strangers to The Rebecca Golding Fan Club.

We don't have to wait all that long, and when it's our turn to be seated, I feel the eyes shifting to watch my mother walk by. There's a guy with his average wife and average kid who might be sleeping on the couch tonight after the way he eye-fucks my mom; there's a table of college-age guys, one of whom literally raises his glass in salute when she walks by.

We slide into the vinyl-upholstered booth in a row: me, my mother, and then Jordan. I wonder if she feels it—the competing pulls for her attention from all of us—the restaurant patrons, the waiter, Jordan, and me, always me. That's how it is with my mother. Everyone wants a piece of her. Everyone wants her eyes on their face.

Mom has turned her body not away from me exactly but undeniably toward Jordan. And they are drinking together, some kind of Asian beer with Chinese letters on the sweating paper labels.

I'm not drinking, of course, because even though Jordan is technically more of my generation than hers, he falls on the other side of the invisible line of twenty-one, so he and she are the pair and I am the kid at the table.

We've placed our orders and the egg rolls have come and soon the main course will arrive. I try not to feel like I'm sitting at the wrong table, but it's hard to be totally comfortable when she and Jordan are laughing about some running joke from the reggae concert and I have no clue what they're talking about.

My mom finally notices that it's been a while since I've said anything right around the time my kung pao gets to the table. She smiles at me totally, sincerely, and I know she doesn't mean to exclude me. Jordan doesn't, either—he's a nice enough guy—but let's face it, I don't belong at this table. There are ensemble scenes, and then there are date scenes. Supporting cast is supposed to fade into the background when the music gets all romantic and the lights begin to dim.

"How's your food, Seph?" asks my mother, and she turns to me in an obvious attempt to make me feel included. After all, this dinner is supposed to be about my newfound (potential) employment.

Right then my phone vibrates in my pocket.

I look down at the screen, and they pick up the conversation where they left off. I recognize the number, even though I haven't saved it in my phone or assigned a name to it. I stare at the bright screen as it vibrates like a rattlesnake in my hand. After a moment or two, it stops. Then another moment passes and it vibrates once more, letting me know that he left a message.

Now that desire that I'd felt earlier, back in the apartment—to have fun—is completely gone.

"Hey," I say. I have to say it again before either of them hears me. "Hey. I think I'd better go back and do my math homework."

Jordan looks—for a flash, before he rearranges his expression—like he's won a prize. Then he does his best to look sorry that I'm leaving, but come on.

My mom fakes it a little better. "You're not even going to stay for fortune cookies?"

"I'll grab one on the way out," I tell her, and I do, in case she's watching me leave, but I throw it in a trash can just outside the restaurant door without cracking it open. Minor players don't have destinies.

My phone vibrates again, and I yank it out of my pocket. It's a text, finally, from Marissa. *Party at Sal's. Bring beer,* she's written, ironically I'm sure, because she knows I don't have money for beer. Or an ID.

So I show up empty-handed twenty minutes later.

The gathering of individuals hanging out on Sal's mom's shitty couch doesn't really live up to the promise of the word *party.*

There's Sal, of course, and Marissa, who seems to have

forgiven Sal for whatever his latest act of assholery has been, and Sal's buddy Blake. I hear the toilet flush, and then Darrin comes out, not even pretending to have washed his hands.

"He-y, Seph," says Marissa, and she unwinds herself from Sal and weaves her way over to me, wrapping her arms around my neck and planting a big kiss on my mouth.

So there were beers earlier.

This is something Marissa likes to do: kiss me in front of an audience. We've kissed—I mean, a real kiss, on the lips, like this, with heat and tongue—maybe six times. I've enjoyed it exactly twice. Those were the two times we *didn't* have an audience.

Tonight is public, not private. Marissa wants this from me, for whatever reason, and she is my friend, my sister, so I give it to her. And maybe it's not just for her. Maybe it's the unanswered phone calls, the image of my mother in her red dress, and Jordan's dogged attentiveness to her. All of it peaks like a wave and crashes. I feast on Marissa's mouth, feeling her lips soften and spread as my teeth press against them, and I fill her with my tongue. I sense them, the others—the audience—but it's not for them that I perform. It's for her and for me maybe too. It feels good to overwhelm her, to give her more than what she's asked for. I feel her surprise in my intensity as her shoulders tighten and her breath catches before she melts against me, for effect or for real I don't know, but it doesn't matter anyway.

My hands go up and down the sides of her body. My leg finds its way in between her thighs. I press up against her, and in a motion that doesn't feel intentional, she pushes back, grinding into my leg.

I don't pull away, so I guess it's Marissa who does, with

shocked wide eyes and parted lips, and it's funny to see her looking like that—off-balance and surprised.

Our audience seems to sense the show is over. They hoot their approval and someone, I think Sal, says something about live-action lesbo porn, and it takes Marissa a moment to pull all the way away from me and a moment more before she finds her voice.

"Didja bring the beer?" she jokes.

"Uh-huh. Keg's in the back of my Jeep."

"'S okay," she says. She takes another step back and smooths her hair. "Drinking beer is kind of gross."

I refrain from mentioning that she's clearly had a few already and say instead, "Lots of things people do are gross."

"But drinking..." She run-skips into the kitchen and holds up a blue glass bottle that I hadn't noticed before, all of her Marissa-confidence back, "...vodka? Now that's some classy shit." She twists off the top of the bottle and pours more than I would into a couple of glass tumblers.

Giving one to me, she holds hers up for a toast. "To us," she says.

I clink my glass against hers. "To us."

***

Normally I'm not a big drinker. I don't like the spins, I don't like to throw up, and I don't like to end up places without knowing how I got there. But sometimes, even if you're totally sober, even if you think you've completely got a situation under control, you can still end up in places you haven't imagined. That's how things work.

So with Marissa and the vodka I kind of figure, control is an illusion. And hell, my mom was more worried about my fortune cookie than my homework, so I decide, *Fuck it.*

I drink the vodka, and I pour us each another.

Around us the gathering begins to resemble something that more closely fits the definition of "party." People start to show up and the music gets turned up and then there are a few drinking games and even dancing.

Maybe inspired by Sal's lesbo porn comment, Darrin throws this gross DVD into the Xbox, and the moans and groans augment the party's sound track. I do my best to ignore the hard jiggling boobs and condom-sheathed cock and bad lighting. I have gotten good at ignoring things.

In my pocket I feel the vibration of my phone three times. Three voice calls, none of which I answer. I don't even pull the phone out of my pocket to see who is trying to get ahold of me. Marissa is here, playing Quarters with Sal and Darrin and Lolly, who for a change isn't working any of her three jobs tonight, so *she* isn't calling me.

In case you don't know, Quarters basically goes like this: everyone sits around a table with a cup in the middle. The cup is half full of beer, if you've got it, or if it's a shot glass, then something harder. Vodka works fine, as Marissa and the others were admirably demonstrating. Then you take a quarter and try to bounce it off the table and into the cup. If you make it in, you get to choose who has to drink and then shoot again. If you miss, the quarter goes to the next person. If you sink three shots in a row, you get to make up a new rule to add to the game. Anything you want. Like, drink and then take off a piece of clothing. Or drink and then kiss the person to your left. Or anyone who says the words *drink*, *drank*, or *drunk* has to drink. Whatever you want. You lose when you quit or pass out. Last man standing wins.

Not complicated and generally not really my thing, but after I've polished off the second vodka, it's starting to look like fun. I shove my way in between Marissa and Darrin.

It's Darrin's turn to shoot, and he misses. Then it's my turn. I miss too, but Marissa's killer at this game, so she makes it. She points to me the first time, then Lolly when she makes it again, and drinks the damn thing herself on the third one, just to impress the rest of us, I think, and it works.

"New rule!" she declares after slamming the cup onto the table. "If you miss, you have to drink."

So pretty quickly most of us go from buzzed to blitzed, because no one except Darrin is as good at Quarters as Marissa.

No one is paying attention to me now, not like before with Marissa when the room's eyes focused in my direction, and that's okay. It's more what I'm used to, and I get to be the observer again rather than the show.

Everyone around me has the lidded eyes of the inebriated and the stoned. They're staring into their cups or at the TV screen or at each other, the same basic expression on everyone's face. It's been long enough now that dinner at the Chinese restaurant must be over. Even if they stayed for green tea ice cream, even if they had another beer, they must be home by now. They must be together, probably downstairs in Jordan's place, and I see him in my mind, pressing into my mother, his knee wedged between her legs. I see him winding himself around and between and inside of her.

We are all getting drunker. Someone should stop this, and

it occurs to me that if I ever sink three shots in a row, I could reverse Marissa's rule, but by the time I finally do, my quarter plinking as it lands inside the glass, I've lost that train of thought. Instead, I call out, "New rule!"

The others look at me: Marissa expectantly, Sal cynically, Darrin hopefully, and Lolly drunkenly. Her blonde braids are askew, tumbledown. I think she's had enough to drink, but that's her call.

"Here's the rule: if you drink with your right hand and someone busts you, you have to tell that person a secret you've never told them."

"I'm left-handed already," says Lolly. "What about me?"

"The rest of you are righties, aren't you?" I ask.

They nod. I turn to Lolly. "That's okay. You're pretty wasted anyway. Just remember to use the hand you always use."

Next, it's Sal's turn to shoot. He sinks it and looks at Darrin. "Drink, bitch," he says.

Darrin looks at me full of intention and picks up the cup with his right hand. Now I feel kind of stupid because it's obvious he's screwing with my rule, but I say, "Darrin, you have the memory of a goldfish. You're supposed to use your other hand."

"Now I have to tell you a secret, right?"

I shrug. "That's the rule."

"I'm freaking in love with you, Sephora."

Okay. Darrin's drunk, of course, and he's the kind of guy who's in love with the idea of love, if you know what I mean. He likes all of it, I think—the anticipation, the buildup, the first kiss, the relationship drama, and even the breakup. The cycle.

So I don't take him too seriously. I smile and say, "Thanks, Darrin, that's sweet."

He looks kind of pissed, but he shrugs.

It goes like that for a while. Most everyone remembers my rule and the new ones too—Marissa rescinds her rule on her next turn, since everyone is obviously getting way too shitfaced. Lolly adds, before she gets too drunk to play anymore, that anyone who drinks gets to choose someone else who has to drink too; and then Darrin says anyone who sinks a shot gets to make out with anyone until someone else sinks a shot.

That's about when Lolly drops out of the game, probably because she doesn't want Sal to kiss her when it's his turn. He gives her *that look*, and she heads into the kitchen to scrounge for some bread to soak up the alcohol in her stomach.

Darrin is the next person to sink a quarter, and it's no surprise when he crooks his finger at me. So okay, we kiss, and it's not terrible, not great but not terrible either. It's nothing like the kiss with Marissa—I let Darrin lead and I follow, and his sweet mushy mouth doesn't ask for much. It's nothing like how I imagine Jordan is kissing my mother, full of passion and depth of meaning. It's nothing like how it had been with Felix. Darrin's kiss doesn't melt me at all, which is a relief.

Darrin, I realize as he breaks away and grins at me, all happy and dopey, is the first guy to kiss me since Felix last winter.

"Why'd you stop, faggot?" Sal slurs. I hear a quarter bounce off the table and roll onto the floor. Darrin kisses me again.

I wonder if maybe kissing Darrin can overwrite what I did with Felix, you know, like when you reuse a canvas, painting something new over something else. Except of course whatever you painted before isn't erased; it's just buried. It's still there under the new layer of color and texture. It doesn't go away.

And whatever you've done before doesn't go away either, no matter how purposefully you ignore it, how many new experiences you try to layer over it. Fairy tales are like this too. Disney makes them prettier and cleans them up, glossing over the gory parts and playing up the princess angle. But like with art, the original stories are underneath. They bleed through. With paintings that have been colored over, sometimes restorers strip away what's on top to reveal the canvas's first picture.

I guess that's like what people do in therapy. Right? They try to peel away the layers of action, of reaction, of feelings to get at the original source. The moment that precipitates everything that comes after.

The girl on the screen sounds like she's crying now, but that can't be right because this isn't that kind of porno. It's just that it can all bleed together, one thing can look like something else.

My workspace has a concrete floor webbed with scratch marks I've made cutting apart boxes with my X-Acto blade. Layers and layers of shapes cut into the floor until there is no way to untangle them, no way to say that this came before that but after this. No way to separate one image from the next. And layered together like that, intractably enmeshed, they form their own picture, different from anything I intended, but all me nonetheless.

No one is sinking quarters—it's like they've all agreed to let Darrin have his fill of me—and Darrin is showing no signs of satiety. He runs his fingers through my hair in a move I'd bet he got from some chick flick, and his kiss goes on and on. I let him. What's the harm? He wants so little from me, just this, my lips, my breath. His mouth is too wet, too soft, more like puppy licks than anything else. One hand drops from my hair and paws at my side, coming as close as he dares to my breast.

Finally, Sal sinks a shot and tells me to drink and, thinking about my studio floor, about lines cut into concrete, about layers of paint and art and painful mistakes, I forget to lift the cup with my left hand.

"Caught you," says Marissa. "Cough up a secret."

Maybe this is what I wanted all along.

I finish my drink and set down the cup with an unsteady hand. Then I look deep into her eyes, their dark cobalt waiting with a mix of expectation and humor. The humor fades as she recognizes the weight in my expression.

"Secret," I say. "I am a horrible person."

A moment passes, and then her face cracks into a grin. "No secret," she says. "I already knew that."

And of course she's joking, but she's wrong. I am horrible. I have become a beast, an abomination. A cautionary tale.

It's only in the absence of sound that I realize the porno isn't on anymore. I look at the screen, expecting it to be blank, but it's not; it's paused. Someone must be sitting on the remote or something, but everyone's too stoned to notice. The movie is stuck on a shot of the girl's face, close up, and I think the expression is supposed to be ecstasy, but it could also be pain or some kind of horrible recognition. A word comes to me— *anagnorisis*—a term I managed to retain from the stupid vocab list in the Greek unit last year. I can see the flash card: "The awareness of the way things really are."

But then the moment has passed. Someone's ass unpauses the movie and the others are back to their game and I push back out of my chair.

"You leaving, Seph?" asks Marissa.

Sal smiles at me and rubs his hand up Marissa's thigh, and he says, "You don't gotta leave, do you, Seph?" and I don't think I'm imagining the intention in his eyes.

This party is over, at least for me. "Crandall at eight," I say. So I leave and they stay and I've spoken my truth, but no one cares, not really.

***

And at home, even before I push open the bedroom door to see the still-made bed, I know I am alone. If I stand very still and listen, I can hear them downstairs. The rhythm of their bodies, the rocking of her hips, the cleaving of her tail into legs and sea-deep wetness and warmth.

The shadow on the wall is mine. It must be, because no one else is here.

Eight

The next day I leave early for summer school, before my mother comes back upstairs. I don't leave a note. And that night when she gets home from work, she texts me rather than knocking on the door of the storage room—where I've been from the moment Crandall released us. I text back that I'm not hungry.

R u mad?

I stare at her words on the screen, sifting through my emotions to see if the word *mad* matches any of them.

No.

A moment later she writes, *I love u.*

U 2.

It's so *upside down*, isn't it? That's how it feels to me. I mess with that image awhile, a mermaid floating tail-up in the sky, like a constellation, her hair a ribbon of gold reaching almost down to the top of a cityscape, her long copper tail too big to even fit entirely in the picture, disappearing into the uppermost edge of my notebook. I smear pastels to make the dreamlike sky, the wave of hair. The silhouette of the city is rough in charcoal.

The problem with mermaids—one of them, anyway—is that they can't have sex. Not *human* sex, anyway—a mermaid doesn't have a vagina. What *does* she have? One tail, not two legs, no cleft, no hidden female potential. I imagine what a mermaid would have to go through to have sex—ripping her tail in two to create a space between, the act more violent than any hymen tearing. And self-inflicted. A choice. Irrevocable.

My phone makes a little sound that alerts me when someone had posted something new to my web page. The screen on my shitty phone is too shitty to really see anything, so I flip open my computer and log on. It is a message from that new follower, Joaquin. *Is this you?* he has written. And he's attached a photo. I click it open; there is my baby pie, my *INFANDOUS*, framed by the coffee shop window.

An artist's work is like her fingerprint.

Joaquin knows my art. Does that mean he knows *me?*

It must mean that he's a local too. I imagine him wandering the streets of Venice, coming upon my baby pie. The composition of the photo is actually really interesting—the way the front half of the pie is washed out, overexposed, and the back half, with one of the jutting legs, recedes into shadow.

Who's asking? I respond to his post.

His answer comes back right away, as if he has been waiting. *Just me.*

Of course this doesn't help at all because I don't know who "me" is. And what is he asking? If the art is mine? Or if I am the baby inside?

I write back, *Yes.*

I would know you anywhere, he writes back, and honestly this guy is starting to creep me out.

What are you, some kind of stalker?

No, just a lover of art.

I type *Thanks* and close the tab.

***

Upstairs I find that my mom has made a salad and mac and cheese—the real stuff, not from a box. There's even half a bottle of wine and two glasses on the table. Screw top—nothing she'd ever buy. But after a day so long and hot and shitty, it's not very hard for me to avoid thinking about who did. Or to avoid dwelling on how things must have gone if they didn't even manage to finish it. The meal feels like an apology dinner even though she hasn't done anything wrong. Still, she feels sheepish, I can tell, which makes me feel bad because I hate it when she feels bad.

I take an extra big helping of the pasta even though I'm not really hungry and make a big deal about how good it is. We eat for a while in silence. She's lit a candle, a squat yellow one, and it flickers between us. I hold up my glass and watch the candle flicker through the candy-pink wine. Through the liquid the flame looks grotesque, hellish. Or maybe that's just me, reflected back.

The door's propped open because it's hot in here. Every now and then we hear movement, either out on our landing or from downstairs, and I feel myself tensing each time, wondering if Jordan is going to pop in.

Finally, my mom says, "Sephora, honey, would you like to talk about it?"

I know what she thinks the "it" is.

And that's something, and probably we should talk about it. So I take another drink and say sure. And she tells me how it's just fun, for a change, and maybe that makes her not the best role model and she's sorry, but sometimes it's fun to have fun, and of course if it really bothers me or makes me uncomfortable, then she'll stop because it's nothing—*he's* nothing— compared to the two of us.

"It's you and me, Sephora," she says, and I know from the earnestness in her voice and the touch of her hand on mine across the table, our fingers woven together, and from the fact that she's said this so many times before—*you and me, Sephora*— that she means it. That I am enough for her.

But she can mean it all she wants. It's not the whole truth, even if she thinks it is. Because no one person can be that— everything—for anyone else. Not really. Her hands do more than hold mine.

Still, I smile as I unwind my fingers from hers. Her nails, like always, are perfect, each a lacquered pink shell, and I run my fingers across them in the way I always have. I let go and smile again, this time into her eyes.

She smiles back and wipes her eyes and says, "I'm practically old enough to be his mother."

"Only if you gave birth at fourteen."

She laughs. I do too.

"Well, his aunt, then."

That's true. She's old enough to be his aunt.

And then some of the tension seeps out of the room like heat, and things are better. We finish our dinner, and I show her the sketch of Coach Crandall in my notebook. She grins and doesn't even give me shit for doodling all over my pathetic notes.

Later, when she heads downstairs to give Jordan a plate of the mac and cheese, I say, "Have fun."

If I watch her through the wineglass, she can be a mermaid once again.

***

Every summer my mother's sister, Naomi, flies me out to Atlanta. Past summers I've stayed for a week or more, but this summer, thanks to geometry, I'll only be there for a long weekend. Usually I dread the visit, which often feels like an extended lesson on "Why Naomi's Life Decisions Were Better Than Rebecca's," but this year I am looking forward to it.

Some distance. I think maybe that's what I need.

My phone vibrates for a call. I must be distracted, because I don't remember to look at the caller ID. "Hello," I say.

Throat clearing. "Annie? Wow, you're not easy to get ahold of."

My recording is just music, he still thinks I'm Annie. I remind myself as my heart beats in my mouth, *He doesn't know where you live. He doesn't know who you are.*

"Felix, hey," I say.

"Listen," he says, "I'm coming back to California in a couple of weeks. Gotta wrap up that sale from my last visit. I was wondering if maybe I could take you out for a proper dinner this time."

I hear the smile in his voice. Apparently, the hole-in-the-wall we ate at last time didn't impress him. Or maybe it's not a real date if the girl's not wearing real shoes.

"Yeah, I don't think so," I say. "I've been really busy."

"I figured. I mean, the way you haven't had time to return my other calls."

The thing is, he's funny. He's smart. He's good looking.

"I don't think so," I say.

Silence. Then, "Annie, did I do something wrong?"

"I've got to go."

"Think about it," he says, and there's a heavy pause before I disconnect.

I look at the empty plates on the table. The candle which, now that it's burned awhile, has dripped hot wax tears down the sides. They've dried like that. It's finally really dark outside, beyond the yellow security light on the porch.

I think about everyone out there—Marissa and Sal and Lolly, my mom and Jordan, the guy who knows my art . . . and Felix.

So many people, all out there.

PART II

The Rape of Philomela

The bonds between women can be stronger than the hand that attempts to sever them.

Once there were two sisters, each beautiful, each a princess—until one of them became a queen. Married to Tereus, Procne became queen of Thrace. And though her subjects loved her and though she bore a son, Prince Itys, her heart was fractured, for her sister Philomela was far away in their homeland of Athens.

Procne begged her husband-king to allow her to journey back to Athens to visit her sister. But Tereus refused, preferring to keep his wife safe at home and with his child.

"You must remain here," he said, "but my heart is not cold to your plea. I shall travel myself to Athens and bring your sister back with me."

And Procne was glad to hear it and thanked her husband with tears in her eyes and gladness in her heart that she was married to such a man, who was willing to travel so far to bring her joy.

But when Tereus arrived in Athens, he was greeted not by the girl-child he remembered from years earlier, when he had married Procne and taken her from her homeland, but rather by a woman—a beautiful woman, one who by comparison made his memory of his wife fade to a shadow.

Here was Philomela, sister of Procne—her hair blonde like sunlight, her eyes bright and clear, as if they saw for the first time. Her shoulders sloped at an angle just so—as if inviting his fingers to trace their curves. Her breasts, not made heavy by babies and milk, were the size of apples, fruit he hungered to taste—to bite the flesh of them. And oh! The nip of her waist, so tight and small, as if daring him to see if his hands could span it, the flare of her hips like a chalice that thirsted to be filled with his seed.

And though he had come to gather a sister for his wife, Tereus found himself now with a new wish—to garner for himself this woman, as if a morsel or a prize.

Her father, the good King Pandion of Athens, did not wish to let his second daughter go, though he had no reason to distrust his son-in-law. "Already one of my daughters is far from me, a mother now as well as a wife, and who knows when my tired eyes shall see her again? To send Philomela off as well . . . it is too much to ask of an old man like me."

But Tereus had an unwitting ally to his plan: Philomela herself begged her father to let her go. "Oh, please," she cried, "it has been many years since I have seen my own sweet sister. Let me go to her—I will return."

And Tereus swore a pack of lies—that he would protect Philomela and that he himself would guarantee her safe passage and her safe return.

And he watched Philomela with her father, watched as she embraced him, and wished he himself were her father, would that he could be so embraced in her milky arms. In his thoughts he imagined what he might do to her, if he could wrest her away from her father and turn her toward his own embrace.

Pandion listened as Philomela pled her case, until at last he conceded to his daughter's desire. And Pandion took his daughter's hand and passed it into Tereus's, linking them. Holding her warm, young flesh in his fingers—at last! But not nearly enough—Tereus forced his breaths to be slow and even, forced his heart to quiet, and forced himself to bide his time.

"I beg of you," Pandion said to Tereus, "return her to me soon. Already you have my Procne and the grandson I have yet to meet. Return to me my comfort, my joy, my Philomena." Tereus swore it would be so.

And thusly, Pandion entrusted his dove to the claws of the wolf and waved from the shore as the ship sailed, bearing Philomela away and away and away.

The ship bore, along with Philomela, Tereus's secret heart, his desire to part the thighs of his wife's sister, this girl just past the precipice of womanhood. On and on they sailed, across the ocean, farther from the safe harbor of Athens and Philomela's childhood.

Upon the ship Tereus was careful with every word, each move measured, calculated in its intention. He served to Philomela the finest meats, adorned her cabin with the richest silks and brocades, entertained her with the lyre, and poured for her cups of sweet wine.

But never did Philomela's eyes heat with the passion he felt in his heart and groin, never did her gaze linger on his form or face. To her he was like a brother, the husband of her dear, sweet sister and nothing more. Never would he be more to her, Tereus saw, and though he tried to woo her, to ply her, and to seduce her, she did not soften.

The journey ended on the shores of Thrace, and Philomela's heart quickened with joy at the thought that soon she would be reunited with her dear sister. But Tereus demurred, saying it was too great a journey to embark on so late in the day, though the sun was still high in the sky.

Instead, he took her to a cabin, remote and distant in the woods, surrounded by old trees so tall as to block out light, so tall as to hide from any prying eyes what next would happen. And in that cabin Tereus turned the lock before turning himself to Philomela. Now his smile was full of canine teeth, and her heart vibrated with fear. Pale, trembling, fearing everything, Philomela wept and begged to be taken to Procne. But her cries were unheeded as Tereus fell upon her like a wolf upon a lamb or upon a dove with feathers dripping blood.

At last Tereus had had his fill of her. Turning to button his trousers, he did not anticipate Philomela's rageful answer to his deed.

"You brute! You cruel beast!" she cried, and she struck him, her pale arms no more powerful than wings. "You have ruined me, you traitor. It will not go unpunished, that I swear! I shall shed my shame and shout your crime. I will tell the lowest servant and the highest nobleman what you have done. I will reveal your soul to the world, and all shall know of your duplicity."

Shaken by her words and by the thought of others knowing what he had done, Tereus pulled a blade from his belt. He wound her hair about his hand and pulled back her head, revealing the line of her alabaster neck, the swell of her breasts, and as she screamed and jerked and cried, he cut apart her mouth until she could not speak. Each drop of blood that spattered the cabin floor screamed grief as it fell, cascading like rain, like tears. And then—oh, even then—Tereus felt the mounting once more of his desire and he took again what was never his for the taking.

At last he left Philomela alone in the cabin with an old woman to guard her and returned to his castle and his wife. Poor Procne learned from her husband that Philomela had fallen ill on the journey and had died, and she collapsed into mourning from which no one could stir her.

But Philomela was not dead—no, not dead at all. For twelve new moons and twelve full moons, she remained a prisoner in the cabin and a prisoner inside herself, with no voice to tell her painful story.

But one day she watched as the woman guard wove, and Philomela's eyes, still sharp and clever as before, learned the trick of turning thread into fabric. And she thought to herself, if something as thin and weak as thread can make a cloth, perhaps too it can spin a tale.

And so she wove, spinning her story into the tapestry, weaving red images against a white background until her story was at last heard, at least by fabric. Then the guardswoman saw it and, horrified, agreed to deliver it into the hands of Procne, which she did.

After Procne had seen what was woven, she laid down the tapestry without a word—for a moment struck as dumb as her sister—and then rushed to the cabin, where she claimed her voice again, screaming and tearing and thrusting her way through the guards to find, at last, her sister.

Revenge is never sweet, not to those upon whom it is acted. Yet still the meal Procne fed that night to Tereus seemed sweet indeed—sweet and savory all at once, the finest cut of meat he had ever eaten.

With a full stomach and a happy heart, the king called out to the queen, "Bring me our son, so I can bid him a good night. Bring me our Itys."

And Procne answered, "You have him here already."

The king looked around, thinking it a game, but he could not find his son.

"Where?" he asked. "Where do I have him?"

Then the queen pointed—without a word—to his full belly.

It was then that Philomela entered the dining hall, and in her hand swung something heavy—once, twice—before she lobbed it into Tereus's lap.

And he saw it was the head of his only son, and he knew at once what Procne had meant that his son was already with him.

He fell to his knees, spewing bile, wishing with all his might that he could vomit back his son, but some things, once done, cannot be undone, and at last he stumbled to his feet, sickened by rage, blinded by disgust, and chased after Procne and Philomela both, swearing he would avenge his son upon their flesh.

The sisters ran, so fast, so clear, it was almost as if they would fly away—and then, they did, lifting up into the air in a beating of wings that sounded out their own fury and betrayal.

Nine

They really do drink sweet tea in the South. And damn, that shit is good. I start guzzling it almost as soon as the plane lands in Atlanta. I text Naomi that I've landed and sink to the floor in arrivals to wait.

So Greek mythology has become one of my hobbies lately, a source of some of my recent artistic inspirations. That and old fairy tales. The original, creepy versions. And there's a lot of creepy shit out there. I got the watered-down version of the Greeks back in tenth grade, in a unit that combined literature and history. The two teachers—Ms. Kramer and Mrs. Austin— were stoked because it meant they got to combine the classes for six weeks and take turns going on coffee runs while one or the other of them babysat us.

Mrs. Austin, the history teacher, tried to gloss over the incestuous relationships between the gods—Zeus and Hera are siblings as well as spouses; Persephone is the offspring of Demeter and her big brother Zeus. Then there's all the other weirdness—Zeus transforming into a swan so that he can seduce Leda (but what, exactly, is seductive about a swan?). It was funny, how Mrs. Austin sort of wanted to half introduce the stories. Like, those crazy Greeks and their crazy stories, let's not look at them too carefully and let's make sure to remember the definition of myth—explanation tales, things people made up way back when, before they understood how science worked, to make sense of the world around them that seemed scary and full of magic.

Is that so different, though, from what we do now? We tell stories to make ourselves feel better, to make sense of things we don't understand. And real life is scary, and it is magical, at least life in Venice Beach. Not always the nice kind of magic, though.

Anyway, Mrs. Austin felt squidgy about the sexy times. Ms. Kramer, the English teacher, seemed to get off on the whole thing. She went into exquisite detail about all the different ways Zeus got with humans, tricking them, seducing them, and then getting them out of the way by turning them into animals, heavenly bodies, whatever worked.

She was kind of a man-hater, Ms. Kramer. She always made a point of calling on the girls first when she asked for volunteers, and more often than not, she'd shoot down a guy's answer even though she would have nodded encouragingly if a girl had said the same thing.

She had been a women's studies major at some liberal college back East, and her agenda seemed to be to empower girls at all costs. Of course, since we all knew that was her agenda, none of us felt all that empowered by her praise. I can't speak for the others, but I always felt belittled by it. So I'd skip the reading and say the dumbest things I could think of to elicit one of those nodding smiles, seeing how far I could push it.

I wasn't the only one half-assing the class. It seemed like most of us knew just enough about Greek myths to feel like learning more wasn't worth our time. There was this one guy, Gil, a complete Venice Beach stock character, a stoner with a collection of Jim Morrison T-shirts and parents who owned a pot pharmacy. He was flagrantly asleep in the middle of class on one of the last days of our Sophocles discussion. Kramer decided she was going to make an example of Gil, and she did the whole book drop on the desk like it was a teen sitcom.

"Now that we have your attention, care to tell us about Oedipus?"

"Killed his dad, fucked his mom, ripped out his eyeballs, the end," Gil said and went back to sleep.

Kramer should have known better. The Jim Morrison shirt was a dead giveaway. Everybody knows the unspeakable shit.

***

That was last fall. Then it seemed funny to me to make irreverent jokes about how Zeus screwing humans wasn't really all that different from the Virgin Mary getting knocked up by God, just to see how Ms. Kramer would spin it. Now things aren't so funny. Maybe that's why Naomi, with her too-long-for-her-age hair and shiny, Botoxed forehead, irritates me more than in years past when she offers to take me shopping right after picking me up from the airport, eyeing my Dickies and Vans and white V-neck tee with an expression that might be disdain. It's hard to tell with the Botox. Maybe she is going for pleasant concern. It all pretty much looks the same.

Naomi's two daughters, Evelyn and Sarah, seem to agree with their mother that a shopping trip is in order. I think they see me as a fun summer project.

They are growing up—Evie will be an official teenager in the fall when she turns thirteen, though she looks closer to fifteen or sixteen. Those Georgia peaches ripen fast. Sarah is eleven. Both of the girls have their mother's blonde hair, with waves like my mom's but without a hint of her copper.

They have only met my mom, like, half a dozen times, and they haven't seen her in four years. That was the last time she visited Atlanta with me. I'm not sure what went down on that trip, but maybe my mom got tired of being a morality lesson that Naomi seemed to never tire of sharing with her girls.

"When you choose to be a young mother," Naomi told Evelyn and Sarah, with my mom sitting *right there* as if she were a wax statue that passersby should feel totally comfortable talking about, "other choices become much more difficult. Like college—that wasn't an option for Rebecca after she got pregnant at seventeen." My mom just took it, spinning her wineglass by its long, thin stem, and didn't say a word. Tongueless.

Maybe it wasn't a coincidence that my mom enrolled at the local junior college the fall after her final trip to Atlanta.

Naomi spoke in the soft lilting tones of the South, even though she was no more southern than my mom. Junior year at Emory University, she met a pro golfer at a sorority mixer. So she stayed, affecting an accent along with a massive hat collection.

Naomi is five years older than my mom, so by the time my mom got knocked up, Naomi, almost finished with her senior year at Emory, was engaged to Bobby LeBlanc.

Okay. Stop right there. Robert is a perfectly fine name, and there is nothing wrong with being called Bobby if you are under eight years old. But any adult man who goes by Bobby instead of Robert, Rob, or even Bert clearly has some Peter Pan issues to work out.

Whatever. Bobby LeBlanc is actually a pretty cool guy. He never complains about me moving into the spare bedroom for a week or two every summer, and he knows more about music and art than I would expect him to. He's sweet with his girls in a way that used to make my stomach hurt when I was younger and still wished my own dad would show up one day—just slide into the empty chair at our table with a cup of coffee, ruffle my hair like that's the way it had always been.

It's Naomi who gets under my skin. More for what she *didn't* do than anything she ever has done. She *didn't* come back to California when my mom was pregnant with me. She *didn't* offer her knocked-up, underage sister a place to stay when their parents told her that the pregnancy conflicted with their family values and that she'd have to find a new place to live. She *didn't* show up for my birth or help Mom with the medical bills that she had no way of paying on her own. She *didn't* tell my rotten, holier-than-thou grandparents that they were assholes. And when she married Bobby LeBlanc a year later, when I was ten months old, she *didn't* invite my mom and me to the wedding. Because, you know, my asshole grandparents would be there to "give her away" to Bobby, and harlot Rebecca and bastard Sephora would make everyone uncomfortable.

So before I'll let them take me to the mall, I insist on restaurant food. That is one of the perks of visiting Naomi; they eat out *a lot*. At home, a meal out is a rarity, and other than the freebies my working friends slip me, I pretty much live on snacks from home that I stuff into my backpack each morning.

I order a sweet tea—large—from the hostess, even though she gives me a look to let me know that taking drink orders is not in her job description. Evie and Sarah wait for the real waitress to show up a few minutes later to order their Diet Coke and lemonade. It's halfway between lunchtime and dinnertime, so the restaurant is quiet and no one but me is hungry. I order some fries and, on second thought, ask for some biscuits with honey too.

Evie stares at my plate with horror, wrinkling her nose as I split the first biscuit, steam wafting out of it, and smear it with butter before drowning it in honey. "You're not going to be thin for long if you keep eating like that," she says, but she says it genuinely like she's trying to help me, not like she's trying to be bitchy.

"I'm not all that thin to start with," I say in between bites, and it's true. I have hips and tits and thighs.

Sarah is eyeing my fries, so I push the basket over toward her. Her eyes flit to her mother's face, and I see Naomi's almost imperceptible shake of the head before Sarah says, "No, thanks."

There's not much to say while I chow down. Naomi asks about my summer plans at home, and I tell her about my brand-new job sweeping up at the surf shop. She is not impressed. So I ask the girls about their summers to take some attention off of me.

"Mama has me taking extra dance classes over the summer," says Sarah. She sounds ambivalent.

"Oh, yeah? Do you like dancing?"

She shrugs. "Mama says it'll make me more graceful."

I ask, "Do you *want* to be more graceful?"

Sarah looks thoughtful, like she's never considered before whether grace is something she actually desires for herself, and Naomi screws up her face in a way that will keep her dermatologist in BMWs for the foreseeable future.

Evie, who appears to be in charge of managing her mother's emotions, something I remember from summers past, changes the topic by saying, "Daddy had a pool installed last May. It's been great with all the heat."

A pool. That doesn't sound completely terrible. I polish off the biscuits and wonder if I can finagle a new swimsuit out of Naomi.

***

Shopping isn't a complete fiasco. It turns out that Evie has developed pretty good taste, though both the girls are a little obsessed with my boobs—they want me to buy the skimpiest bikini in the brightest color, which turns out to be an extra-small hot pink.

I try it on to humor them, remembering how fun it had been for me to dress my mom when I was little. Sometimes she'd let me pick out her whole outfit and even do her makeup and her hair. Then we'd go out like that, to the beach or the thrift store, and even like that, fashioned by an eight-year-old, my mother was still beautiful.

I yank off my pants and my underwear, too, before stepping into the tiny bikini. The whole thing is a series of triangular scraps of fabric held together with four ties—two on top, two on the bottom. There I am in the mirror, and I know Naomi is going to have a conniption when she sees this, all the *skin*, so for a joke I open the door.

But when I step out of the dressing room, I realize I've made a tactical error. It's not Naomi's expression so much as the look in her eyes that clues me in. Evie and Sarah are all, like, "Ooh, you look so beautiful! That color is amazing with your skin!" which is preteen code for "The fleshy swell of your breasts is hypnotic, and we like the way the ties look untie-able on your hips!"

For a moment I feel what it must be like to be my mother— the power of it and the intensity too.

"It's a little much, don't you think?" says Naomi, at last, and I don't want to but I feel embarrassed by my body, by how lush it is in this suit, how positioned and displayed. As her eyes roam my body, I see her expression freeze on my crotch, where she seems to realize that there's *no way* I've got panties on underneath.

I end up with a suit Naomi picks out, a slightly more demure halter style in cobalt blue. Actually, it's the suit I'd have chosen for myself. Then the girls manage to help me pick out a pretty cute summer dress. Not too short. Turquoise.

And just like every year, I have to begrudgingly admit that Naomi is not entirely the devil, though it's tempting to paint her that way. She clearly loves her girls, doting on them, and she doesn't *have* to be nice to me, to invite me and pay for my plane ticket and take care of me every summer. And though we haven't spoken of it, I know the offer is still on the table, though *why* she's offered it, I'm less sure—accumulated guilt, maybe, over her abandonment of my mother? A desire to cosmically set things right, to be there in a way that she wasn't there for her sister?

There would be more of this—the shopping, the restaurants, and the smooth, quiet rides in new cars.

She's a better aunt than she ever was a sister. I think she *does* feel guilty, and I feel guilty too, like I'm cheating on my mother. There's this story I read, a Greek poem about two sisters, one of whom is raped and mutilated by the other one's husband. The married sister's retribution is immediate and terrible, and her first alliance to her sister is all that ultimately matters.

That is not the story of Naomi and Rebecca.

I think it's interesting how the same person can be so different in any number of relationships, as if our skin is way more elastic than it looks, stretching and shrinking around all the different people someone can become—a sister, a wife, a mother, an aunt, a daughter, a friend. An enemy.

Naomi has to do some serious skin shifting each summer to welcome me to her house, even though my grandparents still won't say my name. In her own way, Naomi loves me. She has to, right? Otherwise, why go to all this trouble? And why offer to complicate things further, more permanently?

If I were to take her up on her offer—to do my senior year in Georgia, to establish residency, and to apply to Emory the following fall—how would Naomi reconcile the roles of aunt and daughter?

When I leave on Sunday, Naomi's skin will snap into a different shape. I know she ignores the calls from her parents when I'm in town. Once I was old enough to understand what was going on, I started noticing as she checked the number and chose not to answer when her phone rang. They call often, at least two or three times a day. Probably for little things that don't really matter, like to ask how Sarah is doing in her dance classes or if the girls got the little presents they sent or to pass along a piece of news about a common friend.

Two phone calls a day, seven days a week . . . that makes 730 calls a year. And I've been alive for seventeen years. All told, that's 12,410 potential telephone conversations.

And they have never heard my voice.

If someone hurt my mother the way they have, there is no way I would answer 12,410 of their phone calls. There is no way I would answer any of them.

***

The guest bedroom is nearly as big as our entire apartment back in Venice, but I guess that's not really saying too much considering what a shithole we live in.

You know, every year I visit this place, and every year it doesn't really change that much—maybe a fresh coat of paint in one of the bathrooms or a new couch in the media room. This year it's the pool. It's not the *house* that's so different from one year to the next. It's me. Because every year I see a little more clearly that this is what wealth looks like. This is what we have none of. And hey, that's okay, because I have always been able to tell myself that my mom and I have something that these people don't have. We are best friends, she and I. We would never do anything to hurt each other. We will always be there for each other; we are a team.

But this year, standing by the window of my guest room, looking out on the glimmering pool where Naomi is laughing and splashing with Sarah while Evie practices her best bored-teen expression in a lounger, I feel especially poor. Because if I don't have that—that thing with my mom, that thing we've always had—then I'm fucking broke.

Ten

"Well, we know you're interested in art," says Naomi the next morning at breakfast.

I look up from my pile of cheese grits and bacon (Evie's having cereal, but Sarah avoids her mother's disapproving gaze and follows my lead with the cheese grits) to see where Naomi is going with this. Her expression is benign.

"Yeah," I answer after swallowing. "Art."

"Well, I thought maybe after a swim, we could head over to my alma mater and visit the museum on campus," she says. "We'll want to be somewhere indoors, with good air-conditioning. It's supposed to be over a hundred degrees by early afternoon, and with humidity, it will feel even hotter." She smiles like this is a good thing.

"A museum," I say. "Sure."

It turns out good ole Bobby will be able to go with us. Apparently, 103 is too hot for golfing, even for a pro. Right now he sits across from me, flanked by his daughters. His plate is piled high like mine, lovingly filled by Naomi. She's only a calorie Nazi when it comes to her girls.

He sips his coffee, sweetened and creamy. "Mama says you've got summer school," he says.

Bobby calls Naomi "Mama," and she calls him "Papa." Swear to god.

"Uh-huh," I answer, gesturing to Evie to pass the orange juice.

"Math?"

"Geometry."

He nods. "Lots of geometry out on the golf course. Angles and such."

For a minute I think maybe the conversation is over, but then he asks, "Did it give you trouble the first time through?"

"Not really," I say. "I was just busy with other things. Didn't do the homework."

He nods again. He doesn't say anything stupid, like how I could have saved myself a ton of time if I would have done it right the first time through, which I appreciate. I heard all that yesterday already from Naomi, who is queen of the obvious.

It isn't that I don't like geometry, that I don't get it. I use it sometimes, the basics—in my workspace, in my art. It's just that I hate homework and tests and the whole fake classroom structure. That and the repetition. It seems to me that if you figure something out the first time, you shouldn't be forced to repeat it over and over again, in every variation on the theme, that you should be forced to show *how* you came up with a certain answer.

Because it's the end result that matters, isn't it? What you have at the end of the problem? It doesn't matter what *method* you used or what your *intentions* were going into the thing.

What matters is the outcome.

"Maybe we can fit in a round of golf while you're here, if it cools off any," Bobby says.

"Maybe," I answer, but even though I know he's got good intentions, a day on the green with Bobby LeBlanc is not my idea of a good time. Come on. Why would I want to open *that* potential can of worms?

You know that book by the Russian guy—that book *Lolita*? I'd never read it until last spring, but before I read it, I thought I knew what it was about. A sexy teen girl who seduces a hapless older man. Like that eighties song "Don't Stand So Close to Me." Not the teacher's fault. Not the man's fault. She's the siren. She seduces him.

I think when I started the thing with Felix, I was playing around with that idea. It felt sexy. To be young and powerful, to have tight flesh and high breasts and know what it means when men look at you. I *wanted* to play. I wanted to see what it felt like to wield that power, to be that girl. The one in the music video. The one with the heart-shaped sunglasses.

It wasn't until after I read the actual Nabokov book that I saw things more clearly. Have you read it? If you haven't, you should. Because the whole point of the thing is that the guy— the one who is "seduced"—he's a fucking asshole.

Probably Bobby LeBlanc isn't a fucking asshole. But I can't see any good reason to get close enough to find out.

***

The pool is pebble-bottomed. I dive in and swim to the bottom, pushing all the air out of my lungs, and I sink. Sarah dives in after me and tries to sink too, but she doesn't have the knack for controlling her buoyancy, and she thrashes and floats back to the surface. I can stay down, my empty lungs content for a moment. My fingers brush across the stones and alight on one that is darker than the rest. Most are white and tan and brown, but this one is black. Like onyx. The tiny multicolored pebbles feel wonderful under my hands. They all feel the same.

***

Emory University is gorgeous. The buildings—tall and straight and white. Lots of marble. Lots of trees. The trees—they help, some, with the heat, their long shadows casting relief across the pathways, but they can't do anything about the humidity. Naomi rattles off the names of the trees—oak, pine, bottle-brush buckeyes, tulip trees—as we meander up the path toward the Michael C. Carlos Museum. We can't do much more than meander in this heat.

It's summer, so the campus isn't crowded. Some students hunch under the weight of backpacks, but most people aren't carrying much. A couple of young women pass us, one with a bag slung over her shoulder, another with a straw handbag swinging from her bent arm. They both wear sandals, not flip-flops. The one with the straw bag wears a neatly pressed knee-length skirt and a seersucker shirt, tucked in, collar popped.

I've got my backpack with me, and I'm only a year off college age myself. People passing us could easily think we're a family of five—that Naomi and Bobby are my parents and that they and my two younger sisters have brought me here to start my freshman year.

Evie and Sarah will go to a college, maybe this very one. Why wouldn't they? Their parents did, and they come from money. I'll bet they'll have no problem mustering up the proper letters of recommendation when the time comes.

My backpack doesn't hold schoolbooks. My wallet is in there, my sketchpad, a couple of charcoals and pencils, and my phone. My pepper spray was in there too until the security guy took it from me at check-in when I flew out here. I'd forgotten it was in there. I know better than to think I can travel with pepper spray. Now I'll have to get a new can.

For a moment, I indulge in the fairy tale. I play pretend. What if I *did* move to Georgia for my senior year? And what if I did enroll at Emory the year after that? Maybe my backpack would hold different things, if I lived in a castle on a hill.

***

The Michael C. Carlos Museum is housed in yet another white marble building. Old, but well preserved. It looks a little like I imagine Naomi will in about twenty years. Lots of spackle, fresh paint. Kept up.

It's free for Naomi and Bobby to get in because they are alumni. Isn't that the way it is? They get in free because they had the resources to go to Emory in the first place. Some poor schmo who has to ride the bus and works a craptastic job just to scrape by? He'll have to pay.

More doors open to those who have the keys. Simple logic, really.

I don't complain about it, though, because they pay for my ticket, and I've caught sight of a sign that announces the arrival of a special collection, an addition to the Michael C. Carlos's already-impressive hoard.

"*May 13 through September 1,*" the sign announces, "*Visit Gods and Lovers!*"

"I want to see that," I say, nodding at the sign.

Naomi perks up right away, probably because this is the first time I've shown any real interest in anything since landing—other than fried food.

It's in another wing, but we head straight there, Bobby leading the way. Apparently he used to bring girls here on dates back in the good ol' days. Naomi points to an alcove with a tall window and leans into him conspiratorially, whispering. Bobby pats her ass.

Nice.

I sneak a glance at Evie and Sarah to gauge their reaction. Sarah genuinely seems not to have noticed, or not to care. She's training her eyes on the paintings as we glide down the hallway toward the special exhibit, and she's got earbuds in too, so she's in her own little world. Evie, though, stiffens a little and tightens her mouth. Not a fan of her parents' public display of affection.

I don't remember ever minding that my mother was a sexual creature as well as a parent. Maybe it's because her sexuality was almost always off-limits to others. Maybe it's because we're more like sisters, in some ways, than parent and child. Maybe it's because she's so obviously beautiful that of course she's an object of desire, someone men would want to touch. I love to touch her too, though I haven't much, lately.

I used to spend hours at the beach finding ways to touch her body—braiding her hair and winding seaweed into its strands; encasing her legs in a wet-sand tail, which I'd decorate with stones and shells; and rearranging the triangles of her bikini top to better display her breasts, which I loved and knew without her having to say were off-limits now, though she'd told me with pride that I'd nursed longer than any other baby she knew, until I was over three years old.

If I try really hard, I can almost remember it—lying in her arms, my head tipped back, my hands splayed across her chest, her heavy breast dipped into my mouth as I pulled at its nipple, the warm pulse of her milk jetting into my mouth.

When you are young, you can drink your fill of your mother.

When you are older, others drink their fill of you.

A framed poster outside the double-wide doorway to the special exhibit hall announces we've arrived—*Gods and Lovers*. I let the LeBlancs enter first; they follow the rest of the crowd, going to the left toward the nearest statue. I turn right and don't look back.

The first statue I encounter is huge, made even larger by its subject—it's *Leda and the Swan*. There she is—Leda—taller than I am and made taller by her pedestal. It's hard to tell if the swan is attacking or embracing her. It's as big as she is, its enormous wings too heavy to ever fly, one draping behind its body, the other wrapping around her shoulder. Its neck is curved into a C as one of her arms seems to push it away, but the serpentine loop of its neck is so long that its beak is just a whisper away from her mouth. Its webbed talon feet clutch her thighs, and Leda reaches down between her legs—to stop it from entering her? To help it find its way inside? Back when Ms. Kramer told us the story, I would have assumed the former—that her hand was blocking the bird's bizarre swan penis. But now I don't know. Her expression is ambiguous, with those flat, round eyes that give away nothing. Maybe she likes it. Maybe she wants it to stop. I can't tell. The swan, though, is all forward energy, lustful, insistent. The swan knows what it wants, and I know, from the story Ms. Kramer told us, that it won the day. Nine months later, Leda laid an egg.

Then there's *Apollo and Daphne*. Their statue is not far from *Leda and the Swan*. This time it's the girl who transforms, and it's not to mate but rather to escape. He was a god who lusted for a girl. She was a virgin who wanted to stay that way. So when he chased her through the forest, begging her, wooing her, and maybe even threatening her, she ran and ran. Finally, her strength began to fade, and, desperate and determined to escape, she called to the river god for help. And just as Apollo is about to grab her flesh, she transforms—her arms lengthening into branches, her fingertips flowering into leaves, and her legs spreading into roots. She becomes a laurel tree and preserves her virginity.

She's kind of like a mermaid. Legs cleaved together into something impenetrable, made more nature than woman. There's safety in that. But now she's stuck and can't ever run again.

This statue, by Bernini, shows Daphne at the moment of her transformation, with Apollo almost upon her. Leaves spring up around her, and the movement of her hair suggests it's growing up into the sky, not weighed down by gravity anymore but rather supported by a series of limbs. Her mouth is open—in ecstasy? In fear? In triumph? I just don't know anymore.

I feel Evie and Sarah trailing behind me. They are silent,

but they are there. I can feel their weight and their breath, and they look at me looking at the statues. I know what I see in these statues—beauty and fear and ecstasy and pain all woven together. What I don't know is what they see in me—which of my emotions are too buoyant to stay beneath the surface, what hidden parts of me demand to be acknowledged.

Then I find Persephone, entrapped in Hades's arms. Her left hand pushes hard into his face, and the marble there is wrinkled like skin. His crown may fall if she pushes harder. His beard could tangle in her fingers. His arms wrap around her waist, one hand pressing into the flesh of her thigh, and I think that if he let go, we'd see bruises there in her white marble skin, so tightly does he hold her.

There's no ambiguity here; Persephone is trying so hard to get free that I can almost hear a cry issue from her split lips. I can feel the vibrations of her effort to escape. He won't let her go. He is bigger; he is stronger. He is older, and he is a god. With him at his feet is the three-headed Cerberus, jaws loose, teeth bared, ready to help bring her to submission if Hades needs assistance. But he won't.

She is just a girl.

The sculptures are beautiful even though the subject matter is terrible. That book *Lolita* is like that too. And I wonder about that—about taking pleasure from these women's pain. Of course they're not real—they're mythological—they're pretend, but whatever. It's only because real women were raped and real men raped that any of this makes a connection for people. All around me people look and point and discuss, faces neutral or lit up in delight. Their pain, our pleasure. I wonder—does that make us complicit? Guilty by association?

I wonder—how can sexual assault be a museum installation?

And looking into the frantic expression on Persephone's face, I think to myself—*But it wasn't her fault. She tried to escape.*

I am not Persephone. I wanted to be there. I put myself in that room. I asked for it and enjoyed it and moaned for more.

***

The ride back to the LeBlanc house is quiet. Smooth. Bobby LeBlanc's sedan is leather and steel and money, money, money. I sit in the backseat, in the middle, because both of the girls wanted to sit next to me and it is easier just to ride bitch than listen to them fight. In front, on the center console, Bobby's right hand holds Naomi's left. Her enormous diamond catches the light as the road bends, and for a moment I'm blinded by it—all of it, the sparkle of the ring, the twining of their fingers, the girls pressing against my sides, and the gleaming wooden dashboard.

Gods and Lovers. A whole museum installation about rape.

Sarah's head lolls onto my shoulder. I want to move but stay still. Naomi looks back at us through the rearview mirror and smiles at the pretty picture of us. Then her eyes meet mine.

She's thinking about whether or not I'll say yes. If I'll go home just long enough to gather up my shit and be back in time for fall semester. I'd make a handy babysitter.

Her intention confuses me. And why she asked *me*, not my mother.

"It's so nice having you here, Seph."

"Mm-hmm."

"The girls sure love when you're here." Then, "We all do."

I break the gaze. I look away.

The never-ending greenscape of Atlanta whizzes by. We slow at last, turning up the long, winding driveway to the Le Blanc house.

Gods and Lovers. A castle on a hill.

I imagine what an installation of my work would look like, if someone gathered together everything I've created into one place. Now, it's spread like a trail of breadcrumbs all across Venice Beach, pieces of me to guide me home. Collected in a gallery or a museum, it would be a room full of torn-out eyeballs, sliced ears, severed hands and feet. Pieces of children. Split mermaid tails.

The unspeakable shit. Strewn across a town or gathered in a gallery, everyone knows it when they see it.

Eleven

The cicadas in Georgia make such a sound that you forget to hear them after a while. It starts when the weather begins to cool, right around the time the sun sets. And it's not gradual. It's like someone's flipped a switch, and suddenly the loud insect call is all around you, pressing like the day's heat, invading, inescapable.

Sarah is a veritable encyclopedia when it comes to the little buggers. Apparently she did a report on them for school last spring, and maybe she thinks I'll be impressed if she rattles off some facts, so that night after we gorge ourselves on Bobby's World Famous Barbecue, after the sun is down and the cicadas are up, she launches into a lecture.

"Did you know the cicada's song is loud enough to cause permanent damage to human hearing?"

"I can't say that surprises me," I tell her.

"And did you know that people around the world *eat* them?"

"Oh yeah?" I look at Bobby. "They any good with barbecue sauce?"

"A little crunchy, but not bad," he plays along.

Sarah ignores us both. "And did you know that cicadas have *five* eyes? And that they spend most of their life underground? And that there are twenty-five *hundred* different varieties? And that they were considered a delicacy in ancient Greece?"

"Do they all taste the same?" I ask.

Sarah shrugs. "I don't know. I've never eaten one." A pause. Then, "But did you know that after a cicada is born, it crawls into the ground and it can live under there for up to seventeen years? And then it finally crawls out, just in time to mate and lay eggs before it dies."

She looks satisfied, pleased with herself.

I think about that—seventeen years of darkness, of half-life. It makes me think of Sleeping Beauty, the original one, who spent all that time passed out only to wake up a mother.

The back of the LeBlancs' house is my favorite part. They have this enormous room, the whole length of the house, floor-to-ceiling screen windows on three sides. The screens are interrupted every three feet or so by a tall mahogany post. On the ceiling, five whirring fans stir the heavy Georgia air. There's a daybed on the far side of the porch, made of gigantic rough-hewn planks, its mattress enveloped in thick linen burlap. Pillows are arranged in clusters: gold and yellow and buttery white, and every now and then one that pops with color— red here, purple there.

The daybed is canopied by silk panels that remind me of the scarves my mother has draped across the windows at home. But those are limp and thin, not really long enough or thick enough, and light from outside seeps through them. Here, on the LeBlancs' porch, the drapes really *are* just for show. But the irony is that they're made of real silk and would actually make decent curtains.

Because it's finally cooled off, we eat dinner out here on the porch. After Sarah finishes telling me all about cicadas, she and Bobby go inside. They invite me to join them—"We can play gin rummy, Seph," Sarah offers, but I decline.

I sit with my goblet of water and listen to the cicadas scream.

The table where I sit is made of the same distressed wood as the daybed, as are the benches that flank it and the chairs at either end. A long burlap runner lays down the center of the table, and there's a centerpiece of fresh flowers that wasn't here this morning. One of the "help," as Naomi calls the stream of workers—all black, I kid you not—who flow in and out of the house throughout the day must have arranged them. More help takes care of the grounds, the pool, and the kitchen garden. It's a well-oiled machine, Naomi's empire, and she rules with a firm but gentle hand. She speaks to everyone in the same beneficent tone she uses with me—a little distant, clearly superior, but not unkind.

I've heard her talking to my mom in the same tone and wonder if she always used that voice, even when they were little girls.

My mother never talks to me like that . . . I don't think she could talk to *anyone* like that. In spite of her beauty, which could separate her from the rest of us, making her a goddess walking among mortals, my mom is of the people. When I asked her once about our religious views, she told me, "I'm a humanist."

I looked it up on Wikipedia. It means someone who

believes in the capability of people to be ethical and moral, free of a deity or fear of divine retribution. I think it means she thinks people are good.

That used to make me proud of her, that she believes in people, in spite of the shitty way her parents treat her, in spite of the way the guy who knocked her up took off, disappeared.

Now it irritates me. It seems . . . childish. Maybe even foolish.

People aren't all good. Maybe not even *mostly* good. And some are bad, all the way through.

I am glad that I'll be leaving soon. Alone on the screened-in porch, I feel the wind move my hair as it blows across the porch, rustling the silk panels. It smells good, earthy and full of promise. I don't notice that the cicadas have fallen still until the rain begins, suddenly and hard, like a panel in the sky has drawn back to release it all at once. I'm dry in here, on the porch; I can hear the rain and smell it, but it doesn't touch me.

I wonder about the cicadas underground, if that's how they feel—shrouded, protected, just a step away from the danger and excitement above. What makes them dig up, find their freedom? I wonder if it's something out of their control, like with the Sleeping Beauty Talia, the way her baby sucks out the splinter of flax from her finger, breaking the enchantment. Or do they choose it, decide for themselves the moment they'll emerge?

If I were a cicada and I were underground, I'd choose a moment like this one to dig free. Nighttime. Stars occluded by clouds. The musty, earthy scent of dirt dampened by rain.

I stand and walk to the edge of the porch. I press my hands and my face against the screen. I close my eyes and breathe.

A day later, as we lounge by the pool, Evie says, "I hope I look like you when I'm your age."

My eyes are closed beneath my sunglasses. "That's sweet."

"Do you have a boyfriend?"

"No," I say. "Do you?"

"We're not allowed to date until we're sixteen," Sarah chirps. She's been splashing in the shallow end, in a long shadow cast by the house.

"Not allowed?" I open my eyes. I sit up. Naomi, I see, is watching me to see how I will answer. She doesn't wear a bikini, though she'd look great in one. Her suit is a sleek black maillot. Strapless, so no funny tan lines.

"Boys can be pretty fun," I say.

"Plenty of time for boys later," Naomi says. She can't help herself.

"I like boys," Sarah says. "I like everyone."

"Mama says it's better not to date a lot," says Evie. She is older than Sarah. She understands implications and intentions. She is testing me. "Girls who date a lot don't get to have a white wedding," she says.

I look at Naomi.

Her eyes are unreadable behind her black sunglasses. "No reason to bloom too soon," she says, and I can tell from the way she says it that it's her mantra, something she's said and said and said until it's become true. It's the story she tells.

Blooming flowers. Spreading petals. Jesus fucking Christ.

***

It's a five-hour flight from Atlanta to LAX, but you regain three hours in the air, so even though half a day has passed since Naomi dropped me off at the airport in her sleek silver bullet of a car, it's barely noon when we touch down.

I've spent the time sketching, reimagining Leda and Artemis and Persephone. My headphones haven't left my ears since the plane took off. Along with coffee and a stale biscotti the stewardess gave me, I've fed myself a steady diet of old-school rap.

The landing is a little bumpy, and everyone claps when the Fasten Seat Belts sign finally flashes off. People start unhooking their seat belts and organizing their shit, cell phones out and fingers flying as they text their rides that we've arrived.

I take the moment of confusion to pull out a small silver sculpture I've made out of soda tabs, loose wire, and the pen spring I found a couple of weeks ago. It's a tiny wolf. I tuck it into the pocket of the seat back in front of me. A little surprise for whoever sits here next.

I don't text anyone. My mom is working, and Marissa doesn't have a car. Now that I've reentered my time zone, the party's over. I'll have to take the bus.

***

It's not as hot as Atlanta, but LA's no great shakes today, either. Waves of heat undulate on the asphalt outside the airport. The tall glass doors slide closed behind me, cutting off the last of the air-conditioning. I shoulder my bag and readjust my headphones before starting for the bus stop.

The bus blows, of course, and it's crowded, so I end up having to stand for the first half. Finally, after I transfer, there's a seat for me, and I slide close to the window and watch the flow of people and cars through the graffiti-etched plexiglass. The bus takes us up Sepulveda Boulevard and across Manchester, and then, finally, we turn onto Pacific Coast Highway. There's a long, slow stretch up PCH, with too many stops to count and a tweaker who yells at the driver and gets thrown off and tired-looking women carrying plastic shopping bags and a couple of kids my age who share their earbuds to listen to music.

My shoulders loosen, and my head gets more firmly attached to my body the closer we get to Venice. The rest of LA is this never-ending amorphous blob of people and cars and buildings and stoplights and smells and sounds, and to the outsider, Venice probably wouldn't feel much different, but to me it's palpable. The air shimmers when we cross into the city limits. There's a smell, a sharpness, a rot-life-ocean tang that tells me I am home.

I get off the bus a stop early and wander down the boardwalk. It feels so good to breathe this air, salty and fresh and not weighted down with humidity. A breeze blows in from the ocean.

A cold drink sounds good, so I poke my head into the Smoothie Shack to see if Lolly is working, and she is, but Kayla the Bitch is behind the counter too, looking like she just tasted something rotten, so I just wave and Lolly waves back and smiles, bouncing on the balls of her feet in the way she does.

I watch the waves for a while. The in and out of them. Sandpipers chase each wave, piercing the wet sand with their narrow bills to search for sand crabs before the next wave rolls in. Back and forth they go, stabbing the sand again and again. From where I'm sitting it's impossible to tell which birds are successful and which birds fail. They all look the same. By degrees, I feel the weight of Georgia evaporate from me.

It feels good to be back in our own shitty apartment, even though it's miserably hot and no one is waiting for me. Mom's left a note for me in her pretty, loopy script—*Hooray! You're home! I love you! Back tonight.*

My phone is dead, dead, dead, so I plug it in before taking a shower. Travel makes me feel gross, and I can't wait to rinse off all the strangers' skin cells that I'm sure I must have collected. The tepid water flows down my back and wakes me up a little. I rake shampoo and conditioner through my hair, mixing them in my palm before applying them to save a step.

My phone is ringing when I crank off the water, and I run-hop naked and dripping across the apartment to answer it, sure it must be Marissa calling to welcome me home.

"Annie?"

I consider hanging up but don't. Instead, I stand there, my hair's wet tendrils on my neck making me shiver, my skin all goose bumps and my nipples hardened into little rubber nubs.

"Felix," I say. "Hi."

"Listen, don't hang up," he says, which is stupid, because if I was going to hang up, I would have already. "I get that you don't want to see me again," he says, "and that's okay. Kind of a shame but totally cool. If that's what you need. It's just . . . Annie, did I do something wrong?"

That's what he asked me last time he called. I avoided answering him then, and I do again, now.

"What do you want, Felix?" I walk with the phone back to the bathroom and grab a towel off the hook on the door. I wrap it around me the best I can with one free hand.

"Look, I know you're young. Too young for me," he says. "I get that. But I have this belief, you know? About . . . relationships."

In spite of myself, I am curious. "Oh, yeah? What's your belief?"

He jumps at the opening. "I just really think that whatever the relationship—if it's for a night or for years—you should try to leave the other person better off than she was when she met you. And even though you're younger than me . . . well, Annie, you seemed to enjoy yourself that night."

I remember the cool soft duvet of his hotel room. A nice hotel, nicer than I've ever stayed in. I remember reaching up to him, smiling, and laughing. I remember the way he pulled my panties down, rough in a way I discovered I liked.

I remember the taste of him.

"Do you leave all of them like that?" I manage to ask. "Better than when you found them?"

"Sure I do," he says, but I'm only half-listening. "I mean, I try."

I have not been left better than when he found me.

I have been left.

I have been.

I have.

I.

PART III

Demeter and Persephone

It seems as though the gods should be exempt from pain. It seems that way, but alas—even those above us must do their share of suffering, though it may look from our lowly vantage point that suffering is for mortals alone. In a way, perhaps, gods suffer more, as they have more to lose. They do not have the sweet sleep of death awaiting them, promising an end to pain if not now, then someday.

There was a goddess who was completely happy. Why would she not be? Under each of her footsteps flowers bloomed, grasses sprung up, rivulets of life-bringing water flowed. When her hand brushed a tree, its leaves spread waxy green and fruit ripened to red on its branches.

Her hair, long waves of copper, undulated behind her as she walked the earth. But she did not walk alone, for at her side was her daughter, her muse, her heart outside her body.

If humans saw them together, they had to look away, so piercingly bright was the love that flowed between mother and daughter. Of course there had once been a male counterpart, a god whose seed had ripened in the womb of the goddess, and of that ripened seed was this girl, this daughter. But the goddess had no need of him now, and it was just the two of them, a duet of beauty.

And though mortals needed to avert their eyes or be blinded by this vision, the gods needn't look away. One god looked carefully, seeing what pleased him and determining to take it.

For him it was nothing to take life, and had the girl been mortal rather than god, he would not have had to act to possess what he desired. She would have come to him in time, as all souls do.

But as goddess rather than mortal, this girl would never descend into his realm . . . unless he caused it to be so.

And so he did.

A flower grew, unlike any other the girl had seen. White petaled and luminous, it had at its heart a purple bloom with a scent that called her to it. And when she reached down with her young hand to brush its heart, the earth cracked open at her feet.

She disappeared, and the seam of the earth resealed. The goddess mother heard only what seemed like the hush of wind, but when she leveled her gaze where last she had seen her daughter, nothing was there—naught but the flower, which, having played its part, wilted now, head down, as if ashamed.

In her fury, the goddess demanded the return of her daughter, but alas, the gods turned a deaf ear to her pleas. The earth dried and died under her feet as she mourned, her heart too swollen by grief to pay heed to the mortals' predicament—and without her blessing, fruit did not flourish and seeds did not flower.

The earth was starving.

Made bitter by her loss, the great goddess clothed herself in the skin of an old woman and found refuge in the home of a mortal queen, where she played nursemaid to the infant prince. If her daughter was lost to her, then she would mold a god out of this boy's mortal flesh, and so she clutched him to her breast and breathed her sweet breath into his mouth; she anointed him with ambrosia, and she lowered him nightly into flames, and as the days passed, she filled him with sweetness and burned away his mortality.

It might be that if his mother had not interrupted this ritual—finding them together over the fire and screaming in fear for her boy's mortal soul—and if the goddess had succeeded in molding the boy into a god, maybe she would have overcome her grief, and her memory of her lost daughter would have faded.

But the mother-queen did spy the goddess at her nightly work, and scream she did, and the goddess tossed away her mortal disguise and stood brilliant and blinding in her beauty. And she remembered her own child and left the boy to his mortal mother and resumed her search for her daughter.

At last the earth could bear no more of her grief, and so the gods demanded that the daughter be released from its bowels. But just before she gained her freedom—right before she was reunited with her sweet mother—the girl goddess ate six seeds from the heart of a pomegranate, each seed splitting and spilling sweetness into her mouth, and those seeds destined her each year to six months spent underground.

Now, some say that she was tricked into eating the seeds, that whatever happened underground was against her will, that she returned to the surface and to her mother's arms willingly and white-armed.

But perhaps the girl found pleasure in those dark rooms underground. It may be that, away from the gaze of her goddess mother, she warmed and responded to the underworld god's touch. And when she placed the seeds inside her mouth, when she burst them with her teeth and savored their sweetness with her tongue—perhaps she knew exactly what she was doing.

Twelve

I don't want to admit—to my mother or myself—that I like working at the board shop. For one, I've spent the last couple of years digging in my heels and refusing to get a job. For another, I owe the job to Jordan, and it still pisses me off that he is fucking my mother.

But I do like the board shop. I like the way it smells—of coconut from the surf wax—and I like the way it feels. Riley Wilson Boards is not a tourist shop. It doesn't carry Venice Beach T-shirts or key chains or refrigerator magnets. It doesn't feature rows of tie-dyed bikinis or sarongs. Riley Wilson Boards carries surfboards. Lots of them. Rows of them, actually, and all kinds—far to one side the used ones, with yellowed spots here and there from old repairs. The majority of the boards are Riley Wilson originals, arranged short to long from the front of the store angling toward the back, standing on end like soldiers in a row. Each is signed like a piece of art—which they are.

On the other end of the store hangs a row of wetsuits, ranging from fall to spring, each suit tagged with its thickness, from 1.5 millimeters all the way up to 8 millimeters, for serious cold-water wimps.

My wetsuit is 5 millimeters, and it hangs now in the back of my closet. I haven't needed to wear it since May. But I like the way it feels to step inside its neoprene legs, to push my arms inside of it and stretch them out, to reach over my shoulder to find and pull the long cord attached to the zipper, sealing myself inside like a selkie into her skin.

A small display of Rainbow sandals sits near the front door. On the counter is this ridiculous old-fashioned cash register that doesn't work at all, the only thing in the store that's for looks rather than function.

I like the repeating curves of the boards, the echo of that graceful swoop up the side of each one. I like the light that floods the shop by ten a.m. each day, the way the light gathers in long rectangles that bend up the boards' faces—though I'm only there to see it on the weekends, since I'm still stuck in geometry's clutches Monday through Friday.

I like the way the door to the shop opens—with an old-fashioned knob, not automatically or with one of those metal bars. And I like the door itself, maybe best of all, aside from the boards. It's a Dutch door, painted turquoise, and the top almost always swings free, so air and sounds from the street waft in. At lunchtime, spices from the Indian place next door almost overwhelm me, and I wish again each day that I was rich and ate out rather than brown-bagging it. But though the job is cool (for a job), it pays shit, and after scanning the menu next door one day, I figured lunch would cost me roughly three hours' work—before tip—so I bite begrudgingly into my PB&J instead.

The shop has a forward, thrusting, masculine energy. The arrangement of the boards—tips up—strikes me as distinctly phallic, and watching the customers (almost exclusively men, most between the ages of sixteen and forty) as they examine each board, running a hand down the hardened curves of them, making their decisions by touch as much as by sight, sometimes I have to look away, as if to give them a moment of privacy.

Some of the most expensive boards are Riley Wilsons from way back, still in pristine shape. These boards are enormous, up to eleven feet long.

"Surfing really changed in the eighties," Jordan tells me. "That's when the thruster was designed."

Thruster. I kid you not.

"It's a three-fin system," Jordan explains, as though I'm not a surfer too. "It's totally transformed the way the surfer can interact with the wave." His face is earnest and open, so I don't laugh or roll my eyes or anything. It's weird anyway to delve into innuendo with him, of all people.

So I ring up sales, sweep, make sure the wetsuits stay in the right order, get coffee from the place down the street when Riley makes an occasional appearance. But my most important job seems to be fetching Jordan from the back, where he transforms foam blanks into surfboards, whenever anyone has a question. This happens often, and if I were pulled away from my work as frequently as Jordan is pulled away from his, I'd go insane.

But it never fazes Jordan.

Today when I go get him to talk with a guy who has questions about board length—should he pick a board based on his weight or height or both (I could answer *this* question, but he looks at me dubiously when I give him my opinion)—Jordan has the reggae cranked up pretty loud, even though he probably can't hear it with the earplugs he's shoved in to keep out the dust. He's got a face mask on too, with a respirator and a pair of goggles. Tiny fibers float all around as he works.

He's already whittled down the blank close to where he wants it to be, having cut it first with a handsaw and then smoothed it with rough sandpaper. Now he's working the power planer, my favorite part, because I like how quickly it gets the job done. With each pass, it smooths off an eighth of an inch or so. He's got a weight on the left side of the board to counterbalance the weight of the planer, and he works his way down the right side in a single unbroken motion, peeling free a long, thin slice of foam from the base to the nose. It's almost like riding a wave, the way the power planer thrusts forward, and all Jordan's got to do is hang on and stay steady.

That's how it looks, anyway; I know it's not easy to make such graceful, clean cuts. I imagine it's like the work I do—it's easy for him now, after all the cuts he's made, but I'll bet that sweeping arc of motion wasn't always so natural. It's become part of his body, that movement.

Watching him work, I forget all about why I came back here in the first place, and the guy in the shop gets to wait a little while. It's beautiful, what he's doing. In a way it reminds me of myself when I sculpt, but it reminds me of someone else, too—Lolly. The way she looks as she bounces around the Smoothie Shack, her hands knowing where to reach without her needing to look, the joy she emanates just doing her job. Those two belong where they are, doing what they do.

After a minute Jordan notices me and switches off the planer. "Customer?"

I nod.

***

After work I meet Marissa at the beach. It's six o'clock and still hot. We run across the sand and strip down to our suits, then race into the waves. They're not big or well formed, so it's not crowded, and we can goof off without getting in anyone's way.

The water's not freezing today, though I'd never really call it *warm*, not on its warmest days. I shiver all over as I dunk my head the first time, but as soon as I surface it's okay. Marissa has beaten me out past the break, her strokes strong and forceful. She's always been a better swimmer. I watch her turn back toward me and paddle hard as a wave crests and breaks behind her, and she points her arms over her head and rides it in.

Then her wave is upon me, and I dive deep under it. The water whirls around me, and for a moment I lose perspective of up and down. It's not silent under the wave; the force of the water makes its own sound. I kick hard and resurface, toss my hair back from my face and lick the salt from my lips.

It's brighter on the other side of the wave. Droplets of the ocean cling to my eyelashes and magnify the sun, and the blue world all around me bobs and sways and glistens.

We dry off and flop side by side on the sand and press face-down into our towels. We don't talk. We don't have to talk. Marissa scoots her foot across to my towel and pokes me a little, runs her big toe down my calf. I poke her back.

I drift in and out of sleep and dream of waves and wolves and mermaids. I wake with a start and a gasp. Marissa's sitting up, watching me.

"You okay?"

I don't nod.

I've got a few wrinkled dollar bills, and she has sixty-seven cents, so we split an iced mocha with extra whip and wander back through town, toward her place.

Neither of us has a lot to say, so we walk like that together, taking turns sipping the mocha.

We pop into a couple of shops just to look around. Venice Beach paraphernalia is everywhere—key chains and T-shirts and magnets.

I leave Marissa at her apartment—"Homework," I tell her. She squeezes my hand good-bye, and when she pulls away there's a ring in my palm, with the price tag still attached. It's twisted wire, just a flat star and a simple band.

"Looked like you," Marissa says, and she grins. I slip it onto my ring finger. It fits just right.

When I get back to my place, I don't go upstairs. Instead, I go to my studio and flip the wall switch, watching the familiar flicker become light.

There's my laptop, and on an impulse I visit the page of the guy who recognized my baby pie. Joaquin. He writes poetry, really bad poetry. No one comments on his poems. The newest one reads:

She

Is Beauty

A long wave

I want to ride it

But it's not the ocean

It's the gleam of her hair

She pulls at me like the tide

She calls to me like the cresting sea

I want only to touch her curves

To bear witness to her beauty

To run my hands

To run my eyes

Along the

Shape of

Her

I roll my eyes. Ridiculous. Sappy shit. And in the shape of a diamond. His earlier attempts aren't much better; I scroll back and skim them. They're mostly nature poems and a couple about skateboarding. Nothing great, not that I'm an expert or anything, but come on. This latest poem is by far the worst of the bunch. The earlier poems, at least, were about the world. Reading through the poems, I wonder what has changed in this stranger's life. What's happened to him that now he's writing *this*?

My art has changed too. Before last winter, it was pretty good, I guess, but now it's better. Maybe that's because I'm half a year older than I was then and that I've had those months to sharpen my ideas. Maybe no matter what, my art would be better.

You can't separate what *could have been* from what *is*. It kind of kills me that my art is better now than before. It's darker, sure, but it's more subtle too. It's the art of a secret keeper. It shows but doesn't share.

I'm cold now. My suit is still damp under my clothes. But before I go upstairs, I send a message to Joaquin: *Your new poem is different from the others. What happened?* I don't expect him to be online and to answer, but he is and he does, almost at once. *Yeah*, he writes. *I fell in love.*

Love.

My computer pings as another message comes through. *What happened to you?*

Thirteen

It's Marissa's birthday on Saturday, so even though I shouldn't spend the money, I take us to a movie. A *real* movie, a big summer blockbuster starring that guy who looks like someone took a frying pan to his face but manages to be hot anyway.

We never see first-run movies usually. We wait until they're in the cheap theaters and do our best to avoid the reviews in the meantime. The showing I take Marissa to isn't even a matinee. I buy a tub of popcorn to split—the big one—and we gorge ourselves on it, big salty, buttery handfuls, washed down with tingly sweet bubbles of soda.

It's an action movie that hits all the right notes, more or less, and it ends with soaring music and a rising sun behind the burned-out husk of a car, the skeleton corpse of the villain lying broken out the driver's side window, with the frying-pan-face hot guy kissing the too-gorgeous-to-be-real wife, and everyone knows that as soon as the credits run he's going to bang the shit out of her.

Marissa loves the whole thing, and I can't help but buy into it a little too, even though I know better. It's another fairy tale, just with a higher body count. I see how they do it—the music, how it builds and breaks like an orgasm, the tint of orangey-pink sky, the angle of the kiss that makes our chests expand with that feeling you get when you know everything's going to be all right.

It's dark when we leave the theater. We've abandoned the popcorn bucket on the floor of the theater, along with the soda cup. ("Job security for the service sector," Marissa tells me. "We're helping the fuckers.")

I ask her if she wants to crash at my place, because Mom will be spending the night downstairs with Jordan. Neither one of them has to work tomorrow, and she was silly, giddy this morning about the idea of sleeping in with him, not being in a rush for once. I smiled and nodded like it didn't bother me, and either she bought it or wanted to buy it enough to ignore the stiffness of my mouth.

But Marissa says she can't, Sal's promised to make her dessert, and she's kept him waiting long enough, so we hug and I say "Happy birthday" one more time and then set my skateboard down and head toward home.

I know as soon as I get to our building that something's wrong. The door to Jordan's apartment is swung open, and I can hear shouting from the street. Mick and Shilo, the two gay kids who live in apartment C, are kind of lurking outside of Jordan's door as if they're trying to hear what's going on but don't really want to get personally involved. I push past them into the apartment. I carry the skateboard across my body like a weapon, and I mentally recheck if I remembered to put the new pepper spray in the pocket of my hoodie—I did.

If anyone's fucking with my mother, I'm ready to go to war.

But I stumble to a stop just inside the apartment, because what I'm seeing doesn't quite make sense. There's my mother on the futon, her copper hair spilled forward over her shoulders, long enough to cover her breasts but splitting around her right nipple. Jordan is on his feet in front of her, holding a brown throw pillow in front of his crotch, and there's someone else—another woman, someone I've never met before. She's the kind of woman who must own stock in Avon or something, the makeup's caked on so thick. She's dressed in maroon slacks and this shirt with a ridiculous bow at the neck, like she's a present, though I can't imagine who would want to unwrap *that*. She's, like, fifteen years older than my mom, and her whole demeanor is so tightly wound that she practically *sizzles*, but not in a good way. The words that stream out of her mouth would be considered "bad" in any company, but since she's directing them at my mom, they're fucking blasphemous.

"Cradle-robbing whore," she says. It seems to be the end of what must have been a crescendo of profanity because she's breathing heavily as if she's been yelling for a while.

Jordan looks dumbstruck and ridiculous clutching that little limp pillow in front of his dick, and my mom has tears down her cheeks, but she looks first to Jordan to see what he's going to do.

A moment passes—too long for my mom's taste, I can tell, and I watch emotions flicker across her face—disappointment first, then sadness, and then something else I can't name. Then she steels herself and rises.

Next to Jordan—and with both of them naked—my mom's age is more apparent than it's ever been. Her breasts are softer than mine and heavier, and the tips of her nipples are stretched a little.

I did that.

The triangle of her pubic hair is a shade darker than the tendrils that drape across her shoulders, and circling her hips is the silvery starburst of stretch marks etched into her skin.

I made those.

She takes two steps—one next to Jordan and another past him. She stares for a minute at the woman—I still have no idea what the fuck is happening, but my skateboard has drooped a little in my arms. My mom kind of towers over the other woman, even though my mom's barefoot and naked. There's an energy radiating off of Mom, a strength, and though the woman tries to hold her gaze, she can't do it, and her eyes drop to the floor.

Then my mother looks at me. Her façade is beginning to crack, and I know her well enough to see that more tears are coming, so I grab her hand and pull her out of the apartment, past open-mouthed Mick and Shilo, and we go upstairs.

She disappears into the bathroom first thing, and I hear her crank on the shower. I hear her crying in there, too, and I stand outside the bathroom door, trying to decide whether to stay or to go back downstairs and kick the shit out of the pantsuit lady.

Then I figure out who she must be, and I'm kind of paralyzed.

***

I see the whole situation again, from Jordan's mom's point of view: She heads over to her kid's apartment—who knows why, to drop off some laundry or a casserole, something like that, and she knocks and turns the doorknob at the same time, just as she always does—probably always has since he was a kid. Except this time when she pushes open the door she finds her baby son between the legs of this female, this woman, her coppery hair shimmering like flames engulfing them both, the scent of her in the humid air.

Or maybe she found him kneeling as if in prayer, face buried deep in the ocean of my mother.

Or maybe she found her baby boy, my goddess mother atop him, clutching him to her breast and breathing her sweet breath into his mouth, replacing his mortality with ecstasy.

And did Jordan's mother's words echo in my mother's ears like a distorted playback of her own mother's disowning curse? Did her heart break at seeing me there, in the doorway, witness to her pain?

I don't know. I can imagine. And imagine. And imagine.

A myth is not in the telling but in the endless retelling.

***

The apartment has grown quiet and dark. Mom has shut off the shower. I go to her room and find her favorite yoga pants, one of her tank tops, a pair of panties. I wait in the gloom of our living room, holding her clothes. When she opens the bathroom door, her shadow precedes her, distorted and unfamiliar. When my eyes adjust, I see her hair is knotted at her neck and her face is swollen from crying. She smiles at me anyway and takes the clothes, shuts the door again. Darkness again.

Mom didn't used to believe in a shut door. She'd leave it open while she showered, while she peed, while she dressed. She liked to talk and listen all the time.

"No closed doors," she used to tell me. "The door between us is always open."

But tonight she shuts it, and I know I've been shutting doors lately too—the door between us, the one that was never supposed to close. I remember I'd asked her once, "Why even have a door if we never close it?"

She said, "Because that way we know that we *choose* to keep it open."

***

I can't stay there, in the apartment, looking at one side of a closed door. I head down to my studio and stare at my notebook for a while, flipping the pages back and forth until one tears. I feel like pacing, but my shitty storage room workspace is too small and I don't want to leave. I want to stay here, close to my mom upstairs, so I take a deep breath and count to ten before shining a light on the sculpture that's been my summer project, my newest baby pie.

I look at the wall, at the shadow I've created—a wolf head and neck curved inward, a blank white eye and sharp teeth, too many of them. A scruff under the chin. Two ears pointed backward.

I take a picture—not of the sculpture, which isn't the main point anyway, but of its shadow. My breaths are even now. The work calms me, and I let myself disappear into it as I load the image to my laptop, as I sharpen the lines, amp up the contrast. Then I sit back and look at it.

It's good, but something is missing. A paradox. Something that circles back on itself, like so many things seem to do: a word that speaks of not speaking. From my box full of scraps I dig out a couple of deformed coat hangers. I've got a pair of rusty pliers somewhere, and I scrounge around until I find it. I want to make a word. This is new to me, so I'm slow and not very good at it, and I puncture my hands again and again with the wire hangers and the pliers both. It hurts and I bleed and wonder briefly about tetanus, but I finish it, at last, the word made of wire and propped between the wall and the lamp. I flick the lamp's switch:

INFANDOUS.

I don't even stop to wipe the blood from my fingers before I've got it photographed and into Photoshop with the wolf head. I sit back and look at the screen. Separated from the baby pie, the shadow has become its own thing. The proportions are different than if I'd drawn it; the ratio of white space to black looks off, the placement and size of the letters beneath the image is wonky and slippery. It's imperfect, and ugly. I curve a line around the image to frame it and hit save.

Then I copy it onto a memory stick. The sun is rising. The myth is not in the telling but the constant retelling. This is my story. I want to tell it, not once, not just to myself, but over and over again.

It's time for a field trip.

***

So it costs about five bucks to print one sheet of stickers. If you buy five sheets at this one place I know, you get the sixth sheet free. Unless you're friends with Kai, the redheaded kid who works the early shift there. Then all six sheets are free.

As I paddle my skateboard down the long, broken stretch of sidewalk, money is on my mind. The mermaid tail of my mother, crafted from brand-new pennies. My crappy little paychecks from Riley Wilson. Naomi and Bobby's wealth, the beautiful bounty of it, how everything they own shines new and smart. The easy purchase of my cobalt blue bikini, the extra-large sweet teas versus my poor man's lemonade.

The sun has risen and the day will be hot, but it's early still and the streets are quiet. A couple of bums are rolling up their sleeping mats and loading up their grocery carts for another day. There's a young couple, my age probably, tucked into each other near the entrance to my favorite thrift shop. They're still sleeping, tangled dreads exactly the same shade of brown. Their bed is a broken-open cardboard box.

I paddle by the House of Ink and the Venice Beach Freakshow, both still closed. The Freakshow claims to have the world's largest collection of two-headed animals. I've never been inside, so I'll have to take their word for it, but the whole idea of displaying monstrosities for money reminds me of the *Gods and Lovers* display and, in a way, of my own art too.

Art and money and wealth and poverty and what is fair and what isn't. Casseroles and throw pillows and cloud-soft white duvets.

I think about the trades we make, what we sell and what we give away, and the secrets we keep—both good and not so good—close to our own hearts. The things that can have a price and the things that should not.

On the boardwalk, vendors are rolling up the steel grate doors that protect their goods at night. They rattle and clank as they retract, leaving doorways yawning open beneath them. You've got to do that—you've got to expose your goods if you want people to see them.

I twist the star ring on my finger. Part of the cost of doing business—of *living*, even, is that sometimes people will steal your shit.

My art, I decide, and my stories, these things are mine. Fuck, so is my body, my hair, and my touch. I own these things—all of them—and I can sell them or trade them or give them away.

***

I'm due at Riley's at ten. I continue my slow skate down the boardwalk, stopping once at Carson's café for a mocha and again near the art wall to drink it. Even this early, surfers are out in the water, and nearby at the skate park, the clatter of wheels on concrete sets the rhythm for the day. Not many tourists are out this early, so for now Venice belongs to us—the locals.

I nod hello to a few people I know, dopey-eyed skaters and wet-haired surfers, their skin dusted white with ocean salt.

I zip open my backpack and peel one round sticker from the first sheet. I smooth it onto the art wall, pressing hard to make it stick against the concrete. The wolf winks up at me.

Retelling.

***

At exactly ten a.m. I push through the turquoise Dutch door. There's no sign of Jordan, even though we're not supposed to leave the front of the store unattended—that's kind of the whole point of my getting this job, so that Jordan can spend more time in the back, but he's supposed to stay up front during the morning hours until I cruise in.

I ditch my bag at the counter and head to the back of the shop. When I get close to the door of the shaping room, I hear something, but not the rhythmic scraping of the sandpaper or the whirring of the power planer. And the omnipresent reggae that Jordan's been semi-obsessed with since he started seeing my mother isn't playing, either.

It's Jordan's muffled voice, and he's talking to himself. "*Such a fucktard,*" he mumbles, and I hear a sound like he's punched something and then something else like he's slid to the floor.

I listen with grim satisfaction, like, *Good, you should be sorry, you sack of shit.* But after a minute the satisfaction wears off, and then there's just the grimness left, miserly tightness in my chest and shame in being glad he's suffering too, the way I know my mom is suffering, the way her sadness makes me suffer.

I push open the door. There he is, slumped on the ground, his back against the leg of the shaping table. He's cradling his hand, and there's a starburst dent in the wall across from him.

It's winter in that room, white foam banked up in the corners like snow, a dusting of it on everything—the table, the shaping tools, the beat-up old stereo, the bar-sized fridge in the corner where we stash our drinks. It's in Jordan's hair too, snowflakes of it stuck in his dark-blond waves. Everything is sleeping here, quieted under the foam snow, everything except Jordan's misery.

That's blazing hot and wide awake.

He looks up at me and doesn't try to hide that he's been crying. Tear streaks stain his cheeks, and he swipes at his nose with the back of his hand. He looks like a lost little boy.

"Hey, Seph," he says. "How's your mom?"

I shrug. "Better than you."

"She's better than anyone I know," he mumbles.

I don't agree or disagree. It doesn't matter if she is the best or the worst. She is the heart of me, regardless. It floats there between us, like another flake of snow, or surfboard foam, the question that both of us are asking him—why didn't he say anything? Why did he just stand there, limply ineffective, and let his mother say those terrible things? Why did he let my mom walk away?

After a while I say, "Well, I'll let you know if anyone needs anything," and he nods, and I turn away and close the door, take my place behind the counter.

A minute later, music floats up from the back room, and I recognize it instantly since my mom's been humming it for the last month, ever since the night of their first date—it's a song by that reggae group they went to hear.

"Oh, Mama," croons the singer to his lover over the beat of the snare drum, "You are my goddess. You are my Lover. Let me be your manna . . ."

I trace a finger along the edge of one of my wolf stickers.

Fourteen

It's a slow day at the shop, and no one needs Jordan's help until almost two. By then he's pulled himself together and is back to work on a board. He's prepping it for glassing, so he's got the respirator on and is spraying it down with air from the compressor when I go back to get him. The compressor hisses loudly, and I wait for him to finish and pull off his mask. The music isn't on anymore.

The guy who wants Jordan's help is a white-ponytailed old-timer. Get this. He's a mess because he's finally broken the board he's been riding for the last five years. He brought the pieces into the shop.

"Best board I ever rode," he laments.

Jordan takes a look at the pieces, then looks up at the guy, eyes all full of wonder. "I made this board," he said. "I'm pretty sure this was the first board I ever shaped for Riley."

"No shit," says the old guy. "Well, I guess it's my good luck you're still working here."

He tells Jordan about all the epic rides he and the board had together, and Jordan nods and listens, but all I can think about is that there's no such thing as luck or fortune. Not here, anyway. In Venice Beach, things just circle back on themselves. That's just the way it is.

Jordan doesn't hurry the guy. He listens to him talk about his board, giving a eulogy, I guess, and even though I know Jordan can't really be in the mood for reminiscing, you'd never know it by looking at him.

Jordan is good at what he does. Shaping the boards, of course, but also this part, the thing that seems like it shouldn't matter but actually it does, as much as the actual work and maybe even more. The customer service. Servicing the customer. Seeing what he wants and giving it to him. Lolly is an expert in this, though she doesn't have a degree or diploma, either. Carson and Kai and me too, I guess. Our Venice Beach motto might as well be "We live to serve." Pleasing people—serving them. It makes our little part of the world go around, like it or not.

I'm hanging out behind the counter, doodling on the edge of my Converse. Jordan and the old-school surfer start talking about classic boards. He wants something like the board he's broken, and the boards Jordan is shaping now are different. Better, even, but this guy doesn't want better. He wants what he's lost.

Jordan says, "Let me get you a card, and you can call us next week. I'll check with Riley to see what he's got in the warehouse."

Automatically I reach into the drawer under the cash register and pull out a card for Jordan. I hold it out. When he doesn't take it, I look up. Jordan is standing right across the counter from me, staring down at my sheet of wolf stickers. He's got a funny look on his face.

"Where'd you get those?" he asks.

"They're mine," I say. I'm a little embarrassed because I'm not in the habit of being around when people look at my art.

"But where did you get them?"

"I made them," I say kind of slowly, because it seems like things aren't sinking in real well for Jordan today.

He looks up at me. He's forgotten all about the business card in my hand. The guy behind him clears his throat.

"*You* made them?"

I don't say anything because I already answered that question.

Then Jordan asks, "Can I have one of these?"

I shrug. "I guess." There's a pair of scissors in the drawer where I got the card, and I pull the scissors out and cut carefully around one of the stickers so it'll still have its backing. Then I hand it to him, along with the card.

He pockets the sticker and turns back to the guy, who looks a little impatient now. But Jordan gives him the card and says, "I'll look into that longboard, man," and the guy nods and smiles before he leaves.

***

When I go back to summer school the next day, it's even worse than I remember. They're working on applying Euler's formula to polyhedrons, and I don't understand any of those words.

I try to get the hang of it for the first half hour, but then I'm just *done*, and it's all I can do to keep my ass in the plastic seat. It's too much to ask of myself, though, to stay awake, so I'm facedown in a puddle of drool when I sense a disturbance in the Force and jolt up.

Crandall is leering down at me, and everyone bursts into laughter at the look on my face. It seems like they've been waiting awhile for me to wake up, and even in my haze, I wonder if staring at me is really the best use of their summer school time.

"Pleasant dreams, Miss Golding?"

"Sorry," I say. "Long night."

"I'm sure they all are," he says.

***

I don't have to work this afternoon, so I decide to cook for Mom. Somewhere in my mind is the idea that now that Jordan is out of the picture, maybe she and I will have more time together again. Maybe I can help her get over Jordan. Maybe I'll tell her about Naomi's invitation. We can work it out together. We can work everything out.

I skate to the store and get the stuff I need. I even pick up some flowers—tulips, yellow ones, Mom's favorite color.

At home I roast a chicken even though our tiny kitchen is hellhole hot, and I make a tomato and avocado salad and I chill a bottle of the white wine she likes.

When I hear her footsteps coming up the stairs just after six o'clock, I'm excited like a little kid with a secret, but as soon as she comes through the doorway, I deflate. She looks the same as she always does when she gets home from work—green scrubs, neat bun, black clogs. But her eyes are puffy and tired, and there's a softness in her shoulders, a look of defeat.

"Oh, baby," she says when she sees the food. "That's so sweet. But I need to lay down for a little bit, okay?"

And when she goes into her room, she closes the door.

I pour myself a glass of wine and sit at the table. The chicken looks like a corpse.

***

Later, when it's too late to hope that she might be coming out for dinner, I put the food in the fridge and cork the wine. I'm a little dizzy because I've drunk two glasses, and I trip on the edge of the area rug as I make my way to the couch. There's the door to the bedroom, and I stare at it a while before I knock.

She doesn't answer. I turn the knob anyway and push the door open.

There aren't any lights on, but the room isn't fully dark anyway, thanks to the scarves-for-drapes. Mom's asleep on the bed. She's still dressed in the scrubs, but her hair is loosened from its bun. I stand over her for a minute and wonder if she's dreaming.

My knees are weak. I want so much to climb into bed beside her, to pull the sheet up around both of us, to match my breaths with hers. But I don't do it. After a minute I stop staring down at her and look around the room. There's the dresser, the one we've shared all my life. The drawers on the left are mine. It's a long, low dresser, painted white, with mismatched drawer pulls and a mirror. On the top of the dresser is some cheap beaded jewelry and Mom's collection of shells and sea glass, arranged around a candle on a little round mirror. She calls it her altar, but she doesn't use it to worship anything.

I pick up a few of the shells and run them from hand to hand. When I put them back, I make sure that they're right where she left them. I have always been good at that—putting things back where I find them. It's part of the way my mind works—I see how the items are arranged and remember, without even trying. So my mom never knows when I've been in her stuff.

Not that she'd care. Living alongside her open-door policy is her what's-mine-is-yours philosophy. Though our underwear and socks and things like that are kept in separate drawers, all the jackets and skirts hang together in the closet. She pretty much never wears anything of mine but doesn't mind at all if I borrow her things.

That's how I'd found the picture. Last winter, I'd wanted to find a scarf to wear. I don't know why; I've never particularly liked scarves. I run warm, and we live in *California*, so scarves are pretty much unnecessary.

But that day I wanted to wear one.

Maybe I was feeling like the kind of girl who *would* wear a scarf. Or maybe I was playing around with the idea of what it might feel like to be that kind of girl. After all, I'd been playing around with lots of ideas lately. Most recently, I'd played around with how it felt to be a nineteen-year-old college sophomore named Annie.

At the top of the closet on a shelf was a box labeled *Snowboarding Stuff*. I had never been to the snow, but before I was born, my mom went up the mountain regularly. Snowboarding was among the long list of things she did well and looked beautiful doing.

I had to get a chair from the kitchen to reach the box, and

since the closet was small and crowded, I had to angle the chair between all the shoes, but I did it. I climbed up on it, and I grabbed the box and took it from the closet and set it on the bed.

There *was* a scarf in the box, right on the top—brown knit, with tassels—but I didn't like it. As I dug down toward the bottom, looking for another, my fingers brushed a photograph.

I knew it was a photo before I pulled it free from the ski hats and goggles. It had that slick texture, the special coolness that regular paper doesn't have. It was an old snapshot, folded in half. There was a young man—twenty, maybe, or twenty-five—handsome, with a head full of dark, shoulder-length curls, a mouth full of flashing white teeth. He was dressed in wild, rainbow-colored board shorts and nothing else. His chest was flat and strong and summer tan. His left arm held up a bottle of Corona, as if toasting the cameraman. His other arm disappeared into the crease of the folded picture.

It didn't make sense. I knew this guy. Not the way he was in the photo—not with long hair, not in those crazy shorts. But I knew him, just the same. Slowly, full of dread, suddenly cold enough that all the scarves in the world couldn't have made me warm, I unfolded the picture, smoothing out the crimped line where it had been bent. There was Felix's other hand, wrapped around a slender, unmarked waist. Her breasts were barely contained in triangles of bright yellow fabric. And there was the riot of her hair—goldish-reddish, wavy, and gorgeous.

There she was—before the stretch marks, before the disappointment, before her parents disowned her, and before the shitty apartments. There she was, frozen in that apex summer—my mother.

The Handless Maiden

Once there was a man who was married to the most beautiful woman in the world. Each time he touched her, her beauty vibrated through him like a bell. She bore to him a daughter, but with the birth came his wife's lifeblood, and yet she was beautiful even in death. The man mourned her deeply and resolved that he would not love again, not until he met a woman whose beauty could rival that of his wife.

Largely he ignored his daughter, for she reminded him of what he had lost. Years passed and with them the girl's childhood. When her father looked at her at last, he saw not his daughter but a woman whose beauty did indeed match his lost wife's.

And so he approached her and took her by the hand and led her to his bed. But the girl was horrified that her own father could wish to touch her in such a way, and she fled.

He followed her deep into the forest and caressed her hair, speaking lover's words instead of a father's. Again the girl refused, and this time the man brought forth a knife. If he could not enter her flesh one way, he would enter it another. So that she might never embrace another man, just as he would never again embrace her mother, he used that knife to slice off first her left hand and then her right.

Leaving her alone and bleeding on the forest floor, the man returned home. The girl, most certainly, could never walk that path again. Instead, she pushed forward, her wrists weeping blood, and she stumbled through the dark, frightened by everything, but pushing on just the same.

That first dark night in the forest was full of sounds—the cries and calls of animals, the rustle of wind through trees, and far off the rush of a river she could not see. But though fresh blood flowed from her twin wounds, no predators came to feast on her flesh.

In time, dawn streaked the sky red and pink, and the girl looked down to find that her bleeding had ceased. And though all through the long night she had willed herself to die, she found in the light of the new day that hunger stirred inside of her the same as it had the day before, that her body thirsted still, that her bowels and her bladder called her to move her body through its functions.

She struggled to do the things that before had been natural to her, so easy that she had never considered them tasks, at all. From the trees, birds gathered to watch her wrestle with her skirts; from the river, fish burbled to the surface to see her attempt to drink.

And the animals took pity on her, birds dropping fruit that she had no hands to pick, fish splashing with their tails water she feared to drink herself, lest she slip into the river and drown.

On and on she wandered, until at last she came to the far edge of the forest, and there she found a castle on a hill. She stumbled toward it until she was spied by its guards, who took her inside the castle walls and presented her to the king.

He found beauty in her face and, in spite of her mangled arms, he wished to take her as his bride. Waiting women bathed her and wrapped her stumps in fine, soft muslin and dressed her in a wedding gown, yards and yards of white draped silk that she could not lift herself.

Maybe she wished to marry him. Maybe she did not. Perhaps, having denied the advances of one man and finding herself deprived of her arms, she did not wish to risk denying another.

But they were wed.

This is where the story should end—the girl saved, wedded, and bedded. But this is not its ending.

After a time the king went away to war. In his absence, his mother tended to the girl, but she resented his son's bride and looked with contempt at the stumps of her arms. Conniving, she contrived to break the couple apart and wrote a letter to the girl as if from her son, saying that he wished her gone from the castle by the time he returned, as he tired of his armless wife and wished to take a new bride.

Did the girl believe the letter? Did she mistake the feminine handwriting for that of her husband? Or did she recognize the artifice and decide to leave just the same, yearning to return to the thick, deep forest?

With the help of a serving girl, she cut short the skirt of her dress so she would not trip upon it, and she slipped into men's boots, which the maid tied with double knots. She had her hair shorn close to keep it from falling into her eyes, and she shouldered a pack that did not lace, full of provisions for her journey.

And this time, when she entered the forest, it was not with the intention of walking through it but rather of making it her home.

Some say that when the birds saw her return, they passed their wings across her arms and her hands regrew as if by magic. Others like to think that the fat orange fish splashed healing water on her stumps and by a miracle she once again had hands.

And some stories tell us that once her hands—her lovely white hands—had been restored, so too was her love with her husband-king, and they lived together ever after in the castle.

But it may be that the handless maiden wandered in that forest for the rest of her days. Perhaps she learned to be clever with her stumps and her teeth and her toes. It could be that she and the other forest creatures formed an understanding, that the magpie brought her pretty things and that the friendly fish splashed water in her mouth to sustain her and that though she was not restored to what she once had been, perhaps she at last found a home of her own.

Fifteen

At the shop, Jordan is waiting for me—that's all he's doing—sitting in my chair behind the cash register, feet kicked up, my sticker and a closed laptop the only things on the counter.

"I like your art," he says when I push through the Dutch door.

"Thanks," I say, but my voice is cool. My loyalties are clear.

"I want to use some of it for the shop," he says. "I think it would be cool to display one of your sculptures in the shop, and some of your images would make cool decals. For the boards."

I don't know what to say to this, how to react, but immediately I suspect ulterior motives. It can't be a coincidence that he suddenly is looking for new images for the shop just a few days after the whole thing went down with our moms.

So I shrug and indicate with a lift of my chin that he should get out of my seat.

He ignores me and flips open the laptop and types something.

"Do you mind?" I say.

"I think your stuff could really appeal to the locals," he goes on. "You know, local board shop, local artist . . ."

"You really want to get back with my mom, huh?"

Jordan looks up. His expression is unreadable. "Not everything's about sex, Seph."

I feel like he's trying to chasten me, and I don't buy it. Everything is about sex.

Then he angles the laptop so that I can see the screen. At first it doesn't make sense. It's Joaquin's page, but Jordan is logged into it. And there are Joaquin's terrible poems and links to the images I've uploaded of my stuff—my wolves, my handless maiden, my Sleeping Beauty, and my mermaids.

"*You?*"

He nods, looking kind of embarrassed. "I like your art," he says again. "I'm a fan."

It's one of those moments when the things you thought you knew lose focus and come back together in a different order, with new meaning. It's not the first time I've experienced this particular sensation, and I still don't like it.

"Have you been fucking with me?"

He shakes his head, earnestly. "No way. I found your stuff online, and I was just trying to . . . encourage you. But this new thing"—he taps the sticker—"I think it's really salable."

I remember the way he stared at it, how he seemed surprised to see it there.

"This town is a fucking fishbowl," I mutter. "And no one is who you think they are." I look at Jordan again. "Why Joaquin?"

He shrugs, all little boy now. "Is that how you pronounce it? Sounds even cooler that way."

I can't help myself. I laugh.

He grins too, and I have to admit that it's nice to see his smile again.

"Your newest poem is about my mom." It's not a question. He nods.

"And you shaped it like a *diamond?*"

He shakes his head. "It was supposed to be a surfboard."

I stop myself from saying what I'm thinking—*lame*—but I literally have to bite my lip.

So here we are, still Seph and Jordan, but now we're this other thing too, these other people—me, the artist, and Jordan too is more than I thought he was. He's Jordan; he's Joaquin. He's a shaper of boards, a fan of my art, a lover of my mother. And a shitty poet too.

"What do you say? Wanna make some boards with me?"

It's one thing to slap my stickers around town. It would be another to see my image on his boards—and to sell the boards, for money. It kind of scares me, this idea, but it thrills me too.

Still, I have to ask, again, "Are you sure this isn't about my mom?"

He sighs. "Seph, I fucked up with your mom. And I need to grow a fucking set of balls with mine. But *this* . . . "—he taps on the sticker—"is something else. It's your own thing. Nothing to do with Rebecca. How about it?"

His laptop has Photoshop, and I have my memory stick in my backpack. We open the image, and I watch as he reverses it so that it won't be backward when we apply it to the board. Then he presses Print, and I hear the whirring sound of the printer. There it is—my sticker, in reverse, freshly copied onto decal paper. We wait about fifteen minutes while it dries.

Venice Beach smiles on us, and no one comes into the shop.

"Okay, it's ready." Jordan cuts the decal free from the rest of the paper. We go together into the back room. The board he was working on yesterday is still on the table, and he measures the tip from side to side and positions the decal where he thinks it should be.

"Okay?" he asks.

I nod.

He presses it facedown onto the surfboard, a few inches under the board's tip, and measures again before he takes a spoon and rubs it, in smooth, firm strokes, to transfer the image. Then, carefully, he pulls back the paper.

There it is—my shadow image, permanently affixed to a Riley Wilson original. The whole process reminds me of those temporary tattoos I used to get from junk machines at the pizza parlor, the kind you have to get wet and then press against your skin for thirty seconds.

"I'll glass the board," Jordan says. "And then we'll see if anyone wants to buy the thing."

***

The next day is our summer school "midterm." I fail it, of course, miserably. Crandall runs the Scantrons during our fifteen-minute break and hands them back to us before the end of class. There's mine, with a big red *F* and the words "See me after class."

"Well, you're not doing real hot in here, little lady." He's been flipping through his grade book. I see my name next to a list of zeros and *F*s.

"Yeah," I say. "I've been a little preoccupied."

"Want to tell me about it?"

He looks up at me, and for a second I consider the possibility that his looks might be deceiving, that he might be more than a third-rate teacher on a first-rate power trip. But then his gaze slips—just for a second—to my chest.

I say nothing.

"Do you have a tutor? Can you afford one?"

I shake my head slowly. I have a feeling I know where this is going.

"I could help you out," he said. "Maybe you could still pass."

Yes. Service with a smile.

Maybe I'm wrong. It's possible that he's just a dedicated teacher who wants to help a flailing student. I suppose he might have my best interests at heart. I think about it—about taking him up on his offer, about letting him help me out.

"You know," he says, "I went to school with your mom."

I push back my chair. I stand. And then I speak. "Fuck you, Crandall."

I'm to the door before he finds his words, and when he does, I let them blur into sounds as I thrust through the doorway and out into the blinding midday sun.

Sixteen

The first wolf board sells within a week, so Jordan decides to make more. Lots more.

We've moved the sculpture into the store, and Jordan has lit it so that it throws its wolfy shadow on the wall between the rows of boards. I have a stack of stickers by the register, and I make sure to give a couple of them to anyone who comes in.

The first one I see out in the world is on a stop sign not far from my apartment.

People start making copies of their own and drawing their own, too, and soon I see them everywhere—on the back of bus seats, on the Jack in the Box drive-thru sign, on the bottom of this kid's skateboard, on the swing set down by the art wall.

It becomes a Venice Beach "thing"—something locals get, like an inside joke, and something tourists *want* to get. It becomes cool. Magical.

Riley's happy as a fairy godmother whose girl made it to the ball, and Jordan doesn't have anything else to do but stay late at the shop, since my mom's still not talking to him. So he keeps cranking out the boards, glassed in all different colors—green and blue and yellow, but the best seller is red, red, red.

And I get three percent of each board sold.

One day, Riley's in the shop, totaling up receipts, when I slip through the door. He looks up at me and grins.

"Hey, hon," he says. For some reason it doesn't bother me when he calls me that. "What the hell does it mean, anyway?"

At first I think he's asking me some deep philosophical question. "The wolf? I guess—"

"No, no. The word. What does it mean?"

"*Infandous?*"

He nods.

"It means something that's too terrible to be spoken aloud," I tell him, "but it's kind of obsolete. No one really uses it anymore."

Riley taps the thick stack of receipts against the edge of the counter and grins. "It must be experiencing a renaissance."

I shrug. "I guess."

"People buy whatever everyone else is buying," he says. "People are sheep."

Not all of them, I think.

***

I can't believe I'm doing it, but I find myself trying to convince Mom to give Jordan another chance.

"He's a good guy, Mom, really he is."

We're cruising through the secondhand shop on the corner of Broadway and Electric. I can tell she's starting to feel better because she has an armful of blouses to try on. I've got an old blue lamp with broken wiring, on sale for a dollar. I'm going to break it up and use the pieces in a sculpture.

"I never said he wasn't a good guy, baby." She moves on to the jeans.

"So why won't you call him back?"

Turning away from the rack, she looks at me. "Because I need more than for him to be a good guy. Good isn't enough."

"It's a start," I say.

She smiles, kind of sad. "I think I'm a little old to be satisfied with a 'start.'"

It's the first time I've ever heard her call herself old.

***

When the report card from summer school arrives, neither one of us is surprised to see the F printed next to my name.

"Jarvis Crandall always was a douche," she says and kisses my hair.

***

Summer is winding into fall according to the calendar, but it's the hottest it's been all year. Even at the beach it's over ninety, and the sand shimmers and looks like it might melt to glass.

I'm not a regular surfer—or a particularly good one—but when we've sold the fiftieth board with an INFANDOUS stencil, Jordan offers to give me the fifty-first, for free.

I don't have to think about it before I shake my head. "I've had enough of that wolf," I say. "I don't need to see him out in the water."

"Well, then, how about another board? One of the used ones?"

So I wander over and look at the boards. I'm not a total beginner anymore, and I'd like something a little more streamlined than my heavy, dinged-up Mini Mal, but I don't really know enough to make an educated decision. Then I realize I've got a surfing expert right behind me, so I turn to Jordan. "Well?" I say. "What do *you* think?"

He grins and comes over, pushing his hair back in that way he does when he's thinking about something. "How tall are you?"

"Almost five six."

He nods.

"And you can pop up, right, no problem?"

I'm a little irritated. "Yeah, Jordan, I'm not a *complete* beginner."

He's too focused to hear my tone. He says, "You'll want something with more maneuverability. I've seen that boat you surf. Any one of these"—he pulls three boards free from the rack—"will open up the world for you. They're all technically still a little long, but the extra couple of inches will give you more power out in the water when you're paddling. That way you can save your energy for the ride."

A couple of teenage guys come into the store, and Jordan leaves me to examine the boards. They're all freaking miracles compared to mine. One of them, a Semi-Fish, is glassed in greens and blues with a long, busty mermaid on its underside.

I run my fingers along the curve of her waist, the flare of her scaled hips.

She's pretty, but I don't choose that board. I pick one that's an inch or so longer; I like what Jordan said about the extra paddling power of a longer board. The power to break away.

The board I choose is blue gray and sleek, no graphic except a slim pinstripe down its middle. It's a tri-fin like my old board.

Jordan nods his approval. "Solid choice," he says. "I shaped that one. And if you don't ding it up too much out there, you can trade it in for another when you get really good." He grins. "Employee privilege."

***

At home I grab a towel and slather on sunscreen. Out of habit, I pull my wetsuit from the closet too. I always wear it when I surf—it's kind of a security blanket in addition to a source of warmth. Its thickness protects against sharp rocks and my own fins when I get dumped and roll in the surf and lose sight of which way is up.

But I know the water will be extra warm today, and it sounds good, the thought of the water and the sky right on my skin, so I shove the wetsuit back into the closet and head to the beach.

The waves are stronger than I expect them to be—head-high, most of them, and some of them much bigger. And the beach is crowded with bodies on the sand and surfers in the water, all of them faceless from my vantage point on the edge of the water. Waves lap my toes, my ankles, as if an invitation, asking me to come home.

I fasten my leash to my right ankle and hop-jump through the foam and out into the undulating sea. Then I throw the board into the water and slide belly-down onto it, paddling hard just in time to ride up and over the first breaking wave.

I paddle farther out and then another wave is upon me, this one too big to go over, so I angle the nose of the board down and take a deep breath and duck-dive.

The board is great, cutting clean through the water, and I hold it tight to my chest and breathe out through my nose to keep the ocean from filling me. I pop up on the other side and shake my head like a fish, like a dog, like a seal.

I'm grinning now, and I paddle again with strong, steady strokes until I'm out past the break. Then I sit up, straddling the board and looking around.

It's a fine day. The kind of day for staying. Even though there are a bunch of guys out here, somehow I find myself with a relatively clear space around me. I take a minute to stretch before the next set rolls in.

I link my fingers and pull my arms up over my head, stretch from side to side and enjoy the feeling of my rib cage expanding, my muscles loosening and warming as the sun dries my back.

"Seph!" I hear, and I shade my eyes with my hand and follow the voice to find Marissa.

There she is, waving at me, not a hundred yards away. I wave back and think to myself, *Isn't that the way it goes. A whole wide ocean and still people find each other.*

I level my gaze on the white-bright reflection of sun on water and wait for my wave to come. It's big and well formed, and I know that if I turn now and paddle I can catch it, and no one else is in position to go for it, so I ignore its size and drop to my belly and paddle like hell.

I know I've caught it just right when the power of the swell catches me from behind, pushing my board both higher and forward with a roar of water. I power out three more hard strokes and then grip the board's rails and pop up, my feet springing forward, toes gripping the waxed surface. My knees are bent and I lean forward with the motion of the wave and then I'm standing, each of my muscles awake and aware and working. I carve to the left, and the wave and I are dancing. I think I forget to breathe, but it's like I don't need to, it's like the wave and the sun fill me up.

Then the wave tapers and fades and breaks white all around me, but I don't drop back to my belly. I keep standing as the board slows and sinks until it gets too wobbly, and then I dive off and I open my eyes underwater to watch the light filter through the salt and sand.

It's perfect under the water. I grab a fistful of sand and rub it between my hands. For a second I wonder if I could maybe live down here, if I could be a mermaid like my mother. I think, maybe it would be better that way—easier—if my legs would cleave into a tail, banishing the possibility and problems. I could swim and twirl underwater, and I could be swift and beautiful and untouchable.

But my lungs are burning now, and above me on the surface my board bobs, the leash that connects me to it pulling on my ankle, calling me back to the world.

**

I shouldn't be surprised when Felix walks into the shop less than a week later. Haven't I learned yet how small my part of the world is and how it folds in on itself ever smaller? It's like this one diagram I remember from geometry, not the summer class but the one I took last year. A tesseract. It's a shape with four dimensions, a concept that I still have difficulty really understanding—probably part of the reason I failed the class. I looked it up on Wikipedia and found this 3-D projection. Rendered in three dimensions, a tesseract is a cube inside another cube with all the corners of the interior cube connected to the corners of the outer cube. But that's not the whole thing; it moves, in a steady, wavelike rhythm, the inner cube pushing out of the outer cube, being birthed or breaking free, and then the outer cube becomes the inner cube. Then *it* breaks free, the whole thing a cycle, over and over again. I stared at that little animated drawing for what seemed like forever, watching the cubes rotate, each time trying to break free but never managing it, always pulled back to their roots.

So I'm not really surprised when Felix walks through the door of Riley Wilson Boards. He and I are like that tesseract, whether or not I want to be, whether or not *he* wants to be.

He's surprised, though, to see me there, behind the counter. The shop is busy, and it takes him a minute before his eyes land on me, so I have a moment to steel myself before recognition crosses his face.

Jordan's talking to a couple of girls—tourists who seem to think he's cute—about surfboard rentals. I can tell just from the way they stand that if he wanted to, he could totally nail any one of them. One of them trills, "If I rent a board, does it come with a personal lesson from *you?*"

My boards form a semicircle around the front of the store, the repeating image of the wolf head like a drumbeat.

Felix's surprise at seeing me there changes to an easy smile. "Annie," he says, "Hi!"

I swallow. I speak. "Hey."

Maybe Jordan knows me pretty well by now, because he seems to sense my dis-ease, and he breaks away from the girls and hovers, just far enough away.

"What are you doing here?" Felix asks, which is a pretty stupid question seeing as how I'm sitting behind the counter.

"I work here."

"Right," he says, "To pay all those college bills?"

There's this moment when I could say, "Uh-huh," and then excuse myself and let Jordan help him with whatever he came in for. I could let him call me Annie. But then the moment passes, and it occurs to me—the word I've chosen, *infandous*, is like a self-fulfilling prophecy, like how Oedipus left home to try to escape the soothsayer's prediction, but the more he ran away, the faster he ran into the arms of his own inescapable fate. I think of the looping motion of the tesseract and the pounding freedom of the waves, and I find that I'm done running.

I hear myself say, "I'm not Annie."

His brow furrows.

My palms are slick with sweat. My stomach roils with sick. But I say it. I say the words. "I'm not Annie. I am Sephora Golding. You knew my mother once."

A moment of blankness passes first, his last moment before he understands what I mean. Then it flashes across his face—all of it—confusion and disbelief and horror and pain as his eyes roam my face, seeing everything now—my mother's coppery hair, his own curls upon my head, and more—the way I looked spread across his hotel room bed, the way the duvet puffed up around me, the way I moved against him.

A sound comes out of him, a horrible sound, and he looks around the shop for escape maybe or for different answers, but all around him it's as if there are mirrors—the repeating wolf heads and the word—*INFANDOUS, INFANDOUS, INFANDOUS.*

He stumbles into one of the boards, like he's been blinded by my words. His hand thrashes out and knocks it over and it hits the board next to it and that one crashes down too. For a minute the store is filled with the cacophony of one board and then the next and then the next toppling down, like dominoes, like secrets.

He drops his face into his hands and shakes his head and then, finally, he leaves, running into the Dutch door in his haste and fumbling with the handle for a long moment before at last it turns and opens and then he is gone.

It is terrible, all of it. His face, that recognition—anagnorisis, again—and the collapsing of the boards. The sound of them. The look on Jordan's face and the way the tourist girls whisper and stare. I've imagined how I would feel in this moment. Triumphant. Relieved at halving the burden, sharing the weight of my truth.

But felling a wolf is a terrible thing. Especially when inside the wolf suit is a person. Maybe a shitty person or a flawed person. Maybe not a person you want to know. But a person just the same.

Jordan is scrambling to right all the boards, and the girls leave without buying anything.

"You okay, Seph?" Jordan asks.

I shrug. I nod. I wipe my eyes and nose on the cuff of my sleeve. I picture Felix on the street, wandering aimlessly, seeing everything through this new filter, a haze he cannot clear away, that he thinks he will never be able to clear away. And I find myself hoping that he does find a way. Just not in my town. And not with my help.

Seventeen

As I walk home in the dark, both halves of the turquoise door fastened tight behind me, Persephone is on my mind. I think of how she tumbled through that crack in the earth and how she couldn't know how far she would fall; she couldn't know where she would land. She must have been so afraid to find herself in that dark place, far from her mother and the comforts of home. She must have missed the play of wind across the tall, bright grasses, the warmth of the sun on her face. And it's true she ate the pomegranate seeds, and it's true that we don't know if they tasted sweet to her or bitter. But it's true too that when the time came to leave, she emerged from the darkness into the light of day.

Some versions of her myth say that Hermes rescued her. That's not how I like to imagine the story. I like to think that she climbed free, that she kicked off her sandals and bunched her skirts around her waist, that she grabbed tight to any handhold she could find, and that she freed herself by sheer force of will. I like to imagine that she dug her fingers into the walls of the earth and fought her way up, hand over hand, dark soil smearing her face, rocks bending and breaking her nails.

I like to believe that she made her way out of the dark pit where she had been trapped and that she emerged damaged but free, changed but still whole, and that she followed a path of light home to her mother.

***

There's no moon tonight. The heat wave we've been having has overtaxed the electric system, and the power in our section of the city is out. The windows of the buildings around me are punched-out black eyes, and the day's heat still hangs heavy like death in the air.

When I get to our apartment building, I look up to our door. It's open, and a soft light glows from inside. The window is open too, and the long, silky scarves blow out, beckoning me, welcoming me home.

I'm silent on the stairs, taking each step slowly. My mother doesn't hear me coming. I stand outside the door and look inside.

She's lit the candles—all of them. The tall tapers that line the bookshelf, the funny beeswax ones on the beat-up old coffee table, the candles in jars anchored by sand and shells. A row of candles, evenly spaced, dots the kitchen counter.

The whole front room of our apartment glows and flickers, the flames alive.

There's music on, coming from the tinny little speaker on her phone. It's not reggae, for once; it's the Rolling Stones, one of her favorites, "Anybody Seen My Baby."

Mom sings along with Mick. Her eyes are closed and her head is back, hair waving down her back and shimmering in the candlelight. As she moves with her liquid grace, dressed in a white tank top and soft gray skirt, I see again her beauty, so sharp and bright that it hurts me.

When the song ends, her back is to the door and she stands very still, like she's waiting for the next song, but when the music begins again, it's the same song. Again. She's listening to it on repeat, over and over again, a loop of sound and sorrow.

This time, when she spins around, I step forward and touch her hand. Her eyes pop open, and in the glow of the candles I see the shine of her unspilled tears.

"Baby," she says. "You're home."

***

When you are loved by someone the way I am loved by my mom, you want them to save you. You want to be rescued and made whole again by their magic touch. But love like that—the kind that flows just one way—it's for fairy tales and children. I am not a child.

I imagine Persephone. It cost her and it hurt her to find her way home, and as she forced herself from that slit in Mother Earth, it was like being born again, except this time, she would remember all of it—the pain, the breathlessness, the heart-rending fear that the crevasse might be too tight, that she might be stuck there, and that her bones might turn to dust under the pressure upon her from all sides.

I could tell my mother. She would love me just the same. Instead, I sit with her in the candlelit dusk and listen to the echo of the waves. Our fingers are entwined. When she falls asleep, her head on my shoulder, I slip out from beneath her. I lay her down and cover her and make myself a bed on the floor nearby.

When I sleep, I dream of the handless maiden finding her home in the forest, far from the safety of the castle on the hill, among the creatures who love her. I dream of Philomela and her sister turning to birds and cutting across the sky.

***

When I wake at dawn, she is still asleep. My body is sore from my night on the carpet. The candles have all burned out, down to nubs.

On my quiet bare feet, I pad into the bedroom, taking with me the pack of matches from the table. I slip the photo from where I've hidden it, in the far back corner of my drawer.

Yes. There is a resemblance. In the curl of his hair, most of all, but also in the way he holds his chin and in the way he smiles. But there is more of *her* in me—more of my mother. I have her hands. Her coloring. Her straight nose. And more than that—she and I have things he will never have. Most of all, we have each other.

The picture tears easily, as if it's wanted to for a long time, right down the crease. I tuck away the half of my mother and sit on the edge of the bed and look once more at Felix before I strike the match and feed the flame.

The photo smokes and smells terrible as it burns, which is as it should be. It curls and blackens, and then finally it is gone.

After a while, I get up and make coffee.

Outside the sky is already bright and blue.

The Mermaid and the Wolf

Once there was a mermaid who dared to love a wolf. Her love for him was so sudden and so fierce that it tore her tail into legs.

They met and mated on the sand of the beach. He had traveled from his den in the mountain, and she had swum fathoms from her undersea world. But when they had consummated their love, the mermaid found that the wolf was still a wolf, and she watched as he trotted away, home to his mountain, tail wagging behind him.

She was not alone when he left—not anymore. Months later, she birthed a child, by herself, and in the sea. Her daughter looked up at her with luminous brown eyes, soulful and wide. The mermaid raised her daughter with never a mention of the wolf who had sired her.

The girl was not a mermaid like her mother. She was not a wolf like her father. She was of the sea and of the shore, both— she was mammal and hunter, able to connive and sneak and lie like a wolf, things her mermaid mother could never do. She could create and dance and know the sea deeply and well, things her wolf father would find impossible.

She was a seal, the marriage between a land hunter and a sea dweller, and she was sleek and strong and swift.

Together the mermaid and the seal swam and dove and played in the sea. They slept with tangled limbs on a bed of seaweed. The seal girl watched with awe as her mother wove coral in her hair, as she decorated her body with shells.

But one day the seal girl left her mermaid mother and found her way to the beach—the same beach where years before the mermaid had met the wolf.

And when the wolf returned, the seal girl did not recognize him and he did not guess that she was of his flesh. So they fell together in the sand, and he knew her as he had known her mother.

When the seal girl learned what she had done, she swam far and alone, away from home, away from her mermaid mother. She feared what she had become, and perhaps even more, she feared who she might always have been, beneath the surface.

Away she swam until she found a shore she had never seen before. She lay in the shallows for a long time. She breathed in and out. She waited, and she mourned.

And at last she reached down to her chest and found that just above her heart there was an opening she had not known was there. She used her fins to peel it open, and though she feared she was stripping herself of her very life, she pushed the sealskin back. Her heart beat so quick, her breaths came so fast, she thought she might die.

But she did not die, and as she worked her way free of the sealskin she saw what she was—she saw her own long arms, her fingers, her shoulders, her breasts and hips. Her legs. The cleft between them.

Then she stood in the soft, caressing sea, and she stepped out of her sealskin—naked, exposed, but free.

She took first one tentative step, then another.

And leaving the skin behind her, crumpled on the edge of the ocean, she walked up the sandy shore.

She was a wolf and a mermaid, as well. She was all of that and more.

It occurred to her that she would like to know what she was and who. So she walked on, naked but no longer shamed.

Author's Note

Sephora Golding steps into the tradition of storytellers, sculpting ancient tales in an effort to understand both her world and herself. I am grateful to the source material that informs *INFANDOUS* and encourage readers to seek out the various permutations of the myths, fairy tales, and legends I've incorporated into Sephora's story.

Acknowledgments

This book reached its final manifestation because it crossed the desk of Andrew Karre. I remember the day (July 12, 2013) that I saw your tweet—"Jesus Christ, Humbert Humbert just walked into the manuscript I'm reading. Do that again!" I knew you must be talking about *INFANDOUS*. Your insight from that day forward has been a driving force behind this book. I am a better writer because of our work together.

I am grateful also to Rubin Pfeffer, who came to my house to make art with me and my kids and who sent me a one-of-a-kind INFANDOUS wolf head. Thank you, Rubin, for all of your support. Grateful thanks also to Howard Hornreich.

If not for Erin O'Shea, I wouldn't have known about the shadow sculptures of Tim Noble and Sue Webster. Thank you, Erin, for pointing me in this direction.

Special thanks to Paige Davis Arrington, Melanie Sinclair, Laura Jane Carpenter, Sasha Kuczynski, and Mischa Kuczynski Erickson, who talked me through this book's difficult gestation.

And again, thanks to my family of readers, who support all my ideas, no matter how weird they get. I love you all.

About the Author

Elana K. Arnold completed her MA in Creative Writing/ Fiction at the University of California–Davis. She lives in Huntington Beach, California, with her husband, two children, and a menagerie of animals. *INFANDOUS* is her first book for Carolrhoda Lab™.